"You guys aren't going to believe it," Tia began. "I met with Mr. Nelson this morning, and he told me that I was nominated for the Senate scholarship! Can you believe it?" Tia waited for her friends to explode into excitement with her, but instead they both just stared at her.

"Hel-*lo?*" Tia shook her head. "I'm not talking about some fifty-dollar scholarship here—this is the *Senate* scholarship," she repeated, "and I've been nominated! Isn't that great?"

"Yeah." Elizabeth nodded, avoiding Tia's gaze. "It is. Really." She split her orange in two, then glanced back up at Tia. "Congratulations."

"Yeah, congratulations, Tia," Maria echoed in an equally unenthusiastic tone.

Tia gaped at both of her friends. "Wow, you better be careful," she said. "I wouldn't want you to choke on all that excitement."

"I *said* congratulations," Elizabeth muttered, sliding her orange aside and focusing her attention on her salad instead.

"I *know* you said congratulations," Tia told Elizabeth. "You *both* did," she added, turning to Maria. "I guess I just thought you guys would be a little more excited for me, that's all."

"You're right. I'm sorry, Tia," Maria said, reaching across the table and touching her friend's arm. "I guess I was just a little caught off guard. See, there's something I have to tell you. Um, I was nominated too."

Don't miss any of the books in SWEET VALLEY HIGH SENIOR YEAR, an exciting series from Bantam Books!

#1 CAN'T STAY AWAY
#2 SAY IT TO MY FACE
#3 SO COOL
#4 I'VE GOT A SECRET
#5 IF YOU ONLY KNEW
#6 YOUR BASIC NIGHTMARE
#7 BOY MEETS GIRL
#8 MARIA WHO?
#9 THE ONE THAT GOT AWAY
#10 BROKEN ANGEL
#11 TAKE ME ON
#12 BAD GIRL
#13 ALL ABOUT LOVE
#14 SPLIT DECISION
#15 ON MY OWN
#16 THREE GIRLS AND A GUY
#17 BACKSTABBER
#18 AS IF I CARE
#19 IT'S MY LIFE
#20 NOTHING IS FOREVER
#21 THE IT GUY
#22 SO NOT ME
#23 FALLING APART
#24 NEVER LET GO
#25 STRAIGHT UP

Visit the Official Sweet Valley Web Site on the Internet at:

www.sweetvalley.com

Straight Up

CREATED BY
FRANCINE PASCAL

BANTAM BOOKS
NEW YORK • TORONTO • LONDON • SYDNEY • AUCKLAND

RL: 6, AGES 012 AND UP

STRAIGHT UP

A Bantam Book / January 2001

Sweet Valley High® is a registered trademark of Francine Pascal.
Conceived by Francine Pascal.
Cover photography by Michael Segal.

Produced by 17th Street Productions,
an Alloy Online, Inc. company.
33 West 17th Street
New York, NY 10011.

ISBN: 0-553-49341-8

Published simultaneously in the United States and Canada

Bantam Books is an imprint of Random House Children's Books, a division of Random House, Inc. BANTAM BOOKS and the rooster colophon are registered trademarks of Random House, Inc. Bantam Books, 1540 Broadway, New York, New York 10036.

PRINTED IN THE UNITED STATES OF AMERICA

OPM 0 9 8 7 6 5 4 3 2 1

To Alexandra Gams

SENIOR TIME CAPSULE

Dear Seniors,

Every year the Sweet Valley High Alumni Association (SVHAA) puts together a senior time capsule for the graduating class. Your answers to the following questions will be archived by the SVHAA for use in future newsletters or other SVHAA publications. They may also be made available to your class-reunion committee upon request. Please return your completed questionnaires to Mrs. Swift.

Thank you,
Dara Nguyen
President, SVHAA

Question #1

Where do you see yourself five years from now?

TIA RAMIREZ

FIVE YEARS? YOU'VE GOT TO BE KIDDING! I DON'T EVEN KNOW WHAT I'LL BE DOING FIVE MINUTES FROM NOW. BUT THAT'S WHAT KEEPS LIFE INTERESTING, RIGHT? OKAY, SO IT MIGHT BE NICE IF I HAD A CLUE ABOUT WHERE I WANTED TO GO TO COLLEGE OR WHAT I WANTED TO DO—OR EVEN WHERE I'M GOING TO GET THE MONEY TO PAY FOR ANY OF IT—BUT PLANNING THINGS OUT LIKE THAT JUST ISN'T MY STYLE. SO ANYWAY, IF YOU WANT TO KNOW WHERE I'LL BE OR WHAT I'LL BE DOING IN FIVE YEARS, I GUESS YOU'LL JUST HAVE TO LOOK ME UP THEN.

Elizabeth Wakefield

I'll have just finished my BA in creative writing at Stanford—or maybe Harvard; I'm not sure yet—and I'll be sharing a really cool studio apartment with Jess (~~or maybe even Conner, who knows?~~) in San Francisco. It will be a huge, airy place with wood floors, lots of windows, and a great view of the Golden Gate Bridge, and Jessica and I will both be working nights, waiting tables at some posh restaurant—Jess while she waits for her big acting break, and me while I spend all my free time working on my first novel (which will be an international best-seller). And I'll only take breaks from my writing to sip cappuccino with my close friends ~~or maybe to go to Conner's latest gig, wherever it is. I'm sure he'll be a pretty successful musician by then.~~

Maria Slater

I'll have just graduated from Yale with a major in political science and a minor in African American studies. I'll be getting ready to start at Yale Law, where I'll concentrate on civil-rights legislation. Do you need to know where we'll be in ten years? Because I have that mapped out already too.

Jade Wu

Not here, I can tell you that much. I may still be living in California, maybe even with my mom, but we won't be in the same tiny apartment we're in now. We'll have a real house, with a front yard and everything. Maybe even a dog. And my mom won't have to work two jobs anymore because we'll both be working full-time and making tons of money. But the best part will be that we won't have to rely on those child-support checks from my father anymore—not that he sends them that often anyway. And if we don't have to worry about his money, then I won't ever have to fake my way through a friendly conversation with him again.

Okay, this isn't really something I want to put in the official time capsule. Maybe I should throw this out and start over.

Will Simmons

Finishing my last year at U Michigan and hopefully having a shot at getting drafted by an NFL team. I'll have to get over this stupid injury and start walking again before any of that can happen—but I'm going to do it. And when I do, Melissa's going to be sorry she ditched me.

CHAPTER 1
MAJOR PRESSURE

Mr. Nelson coughed, then finally glanced up from the numerous papers spread out on his desk. Tia couldn't take her eyes from the huge file folder marked *Ramirez, Tia J.*, in black permanent marker lying beside the papers.

"Well, Tia—your transcript looks good," Mr. Nelson finally said. Tia let out a breath she hadn't realized she was holding. "Quite impressive, actually," he added, peering over the top of his gold-rimmed spectacles, his eyebrows raised.

Tia smiled back weakly. As encouraging as his words were, it was hard to get too excited when she still had no idea how she'd afford college—and so far Mr. Nelson hadn't been any help at all on that end. It was as if he'd skipped the page in her file where it explained that she was the second oldest of five children. So unless Mr. Nelson was about to show her a particular grove of trees where money *did* grow, Tia wasn't sure why they were even having this meeting.

"Tia?" Mr. Nelson prodded. "Are you still with me?"

"Oh, yeah, sorry," Tia apologized. "I was just thinking about . . . never mind," she finished with a wave of her hand.

"As I was saying," Mr. Nelson continued, clearing his throat. "Your cumulative GPA is right around 3.6, your combined SAT scores broke that key 1200 barrier, and with all of these extracurriculars you should be able to choose from a wide range of schools, which brings me to an exciting topic—the Lydia G. Senate scholarship." Mr. Nelson smiled as he slid a handful of papers that were neatly clipped together across his desk to Tia.

"The Senate scholarship?" Tia echoed, tugging on her long, flowery skirt as she leaned forward.

"Yes," Mr. Nelson said, nodding. He sat back in his chair and clasped his hands behind his head. "It's a rather prestigious award. Have you heard of it?"

Heard of it? Maria and Elizabeth had babbled about the scholarship practically since she'd met them, and if Tia remembered correctly, it was a full scholarship—four years of tuition, room and board, and even books paid for.

Tia gave her head a slight shake. Mr. Nelson couldn't be talking about *her* getting the scholarship. "Don't you have to be nominated for that?" she asked. "Like, by the faculty or something?"

"Yes. And you were," Mr. Nelson said, giving her a rare smile. "You and four of your classmates, although I can't tell you who the others are because I haven't notified them yet. Actually, many students fit the basic eligibility requirements this year, but since Mrs. Senate stipulates that there must be five finalists, the faculty had to choose five girls—she always gives the award to a female student, you see—who have really demonstrated an extraordinary ability to shine under pressure, which you have this year."

Tia shook her head again and stared at the forms in front of her. The Lydia G. Senate scholarship. She didn't know too much about it, but she knew enough to realize that just being nominated was beyond amazing.

"Wow," she said, suddenly finding it difficult to sit still. "So, like, I was real*ly* nominated for this? I mean, by my teachers? *Me?*" Mr. Nelson nodded. Tia felt like jumping out of her seat and doing her own version of a touchdown dance right there in the middle of Mr. Nelson's office, but she resisted the urge. Because even more than she wanted to dance, she wanted to get started. "Okay, so what do I need to do now?" she asked, beginning to scan through the packet Mr. Nelson had given her.

"Well, it's a pretty quick process," Mr. Nelson said, referring to a piece of paper from the folder. "Let's see . . . the nominees will all be notified today, along with the student judges."

"Student judges?" Tia asked.

"Yes. Just as five of you were nominated for the scholarship, five students were selected to help judge the competition. In fact, there's a group-panel interview with the student board tomorrow during periods five and six, at which you'll need to submit all of your materials, including two teacher recommendations, a very brief essay, and the application itself."

Tomorrow? Tia thought. *As in, twenty-four hours from now?*

"Then on Friday night," Mr. Nelson continued, "there will be a dinner at Mrs. Senate's house for all of the nominees, their parents, and the student and faculty judges, and that's where the winner will be announced."

Tia felt her dark eyes widen. "Hello?" she said. "Pretty quick? Sounds more like warp speed to me."

Mr. Nelson chuckled. "I know. It's a lot to ask—from both the teachers and the students—but that's the way Mrs. Senate likes it. She seems to think the short deadline gives her a truer picture of the nominees. As she puts it, 'It gives them less time to improve upon their images.' " He shrugged. "Maybe she's right."

"Yeah, maybe," Tia agreed. And maybe, if Mrs. Senate was looking for a what-you-see-is-what-you-get kind of candidate, Tia had a shot. She glanced down at her papers again, still blown away by the fact that she—Tia Ramirez—had been nominated for the Senate scholarship. Four years of college, totally paid for!

"Oh—there are a few conditions you should be

aware of too," Mr. Nelson said, pointing to the front page of Tia's packet. "The winner is required to attend a prestigious school—there's a listing of acceptable options on the last page. And while there the winner must participate in a minimum of six activities, including a community leadership program, and maintain a GPA of 3.5 or higher. Otherwise the scholarship is rescinded."

Tia's jaw dropped. *Six activities? 3.5 or better?*

"I know, I know," Mr. Nelson said. "It's pretty strict, but when you think about it, you've done all of that here."

Tia squinted. "That's true, I guess," she agreed. But still—it was one thing *choosing* to load herself down like that in high school, but she had no idea what college would be like. What if there weren't six activities she wanted to join? What if she slipped up in one or two classes? That was some major pressure.

She flipped through the pamphlet, searching for the list of "acceptable options." When she found it, she scanned the names, relieved that they weren't all Ivy League schools like Harvard or Yale—although both of them appeared.

Where's Berkeley? she wondered. She recognized most of the colleges, but weren't they all . . . ?

"Mr. Nelson," she said, scooting forward on her chair, "are all of these schools on the East Coast?"

"Yes," he replied. "Mrs. Senate wants to help

someone else who has the same desire she did to travel across the country for college."

Tia sat back, stunned. She hadn't even thought about going that far away. Could she handle it?

Mr. Nelson stood, and Tia got up too. "Well, I think that's all I needed to go over with you today," he said, gathering all the loose papers on his desk and stuffing them back into Tia's folder. Tia nodded, still shell-shocked by the whole idea of the Senate scholarship. "But I would like you to do me a favor."

Tia scrunched her eyebrows together. "Sure—what?" she asked.

Mr. Nelson looked her directly in the eye. "Start looking at some of these East Coast schools—*really* looking. And forget about the price tag for a while."

Tia smiled. "I will," she assured him, turning to go. He was right. It was about time she started seriously thinking about where she wanted to go to school. But could she really move that far away from her family? It didn't seem possible, but as she began walking toward her locker, one word stayed in her mind—*free.* How could she turn down an opportunity like that? Four years, all expenses paid, at a great college.

Maybe it *was* time Tia considered spending some time on the East Coast—especially if Mrs. Senate was willing to foot the bill.

"That's it, Will," Dr. Goldstein said. "Just a little farther."

Will groaned and tensed his upper body. *Just a few more steps*, he told himself, summoning all his strength. Then, with a guttural moan, he gripped the parallel bars and forced himself to bear down on his right leg, then his left, one foot in front of the other to the end of the mat. His muscles felt like putty, but he couldn't give up now. He was almost there—he had to keep pushing.

"There," he grunted, reaching the end. He used his last bit of energy to lower himself onto the cool metal stool the physical therapist had positioned behind him, then slumped forward and let out a deep sigh.

"That was worse than football practice the day after a loss," he said, breathing heavily. He wiped his forehead and hands with the white towel that was perpetually around his neck at these sessions, then tossed it toward the mesh laundry bag.

"Nice shot," Dr. Goldstein said, gesturing to where Will's towel had landed, directly on top of the sack.

"Yeah, well, the arm's not the problem," Will said, staring down at his battered knee. It was throbbing with pain so intense, Will thought he should be able to see it swell and contract right before his eyes. Instead it just looked red, inflated, and useless.

"No, your arm's not the problem," Dr. Goldstein agreed, "but your leg isn't doing too badly either." She trained her encouraging blue eyes on Will, but he glanced away. *Tell that to the U Michigan scout,* he thought bitterly. Hank Krubowski certainly wasn't hanging around waiting for Will to get better. But then again, who was? Even Melissa had traded up. Will gritted his teeth at the thought of Melissa leaving him for Ken Matthews. It still blew him away that she could be so shallow—especially after he had stood by her through crisis after crisis.

"Really, Will," Dr. Goldstein continued, her steady voice commanding his attention. "You're doing quite well—better than most people with this kind of injury."

Will turned his head slowly, focusing on the dark blue lettering of Dr. Goldstein's name tag against her white lab coat. "Yeah?" he asked, reluctantly meeting her eyes.

Dr. Goldstein nodded, a wide smile stretching across her face. "Yes, really," she told him. "Most people take at least a month to make this kind of progress. Your determination is admirable."

For the first time in weeks Will felt a smile creeping onto his face. If he was that far ahead already, he could definitely get back on the field. He might even still have a shot at that scholarship. Will's confidence began to soar—until he took another peek at Dr. Goldstein's expression. That familiar note of caution was in her eyes, the look she got right before launching into one of her warnings.

Don't set your goals too high, Will. Let's just take it one day at a time. There were a thousand more phrases like that, and Will had heard them all. From Dr. Goldstein, from his parents, from every single doctor or therapist that had consulted with him since his injury.

"Thanks," Will said flatly, keeping his smile in check. "I'm just trying to get better."

"And you will." Dr. Goldstein nodded. *"In time."* Will rolled his eyes—unable to stop himself in time, but luckily Dr. Goldstein was focused on her daily planner. "So, we'll see you again on Friday morning, ten A.M., right?" she asked, looking up briefly.

"Right," Will agreed. It was hard to believe it had been only a couple of weeks since he'd started coming to these sessions.

Dr. Goldstein scribbled something down in her notebook, then headed for the door. "Back in a minute," she said as she darted out of the room. Will nodded. He knew the routine. She was going to get Will's mother, who would be patiently waiting in the reception area, flipping through an outdated copy of *People* or *Newsweek*.

"In time," Will mimicked when she was out of earshot. He stared at his reflection in the mirror. "She had to say it, didn't she?" he muttered. He let his gaze wander around the room. With all of the mirrors and bars along the walls, the place looked more like a ballet studio than a rehabilitation facility. Or at least it would if it weren't for all of the treadmills, stationary bikes, and large colored balls.

Will glanced back at the open doorway, where his mother would be standing soon, his wheelchair in front of her. He hated that stupid chair, and he didn't need it. He could get around just fine on crutches, even if he did fall once in a while, but his mom and Dr. Goldstein always insisted on using the chair after PT sessions. *You don't want to overexert yourself, do you?* Will rolled his eyes again. He knew everyone was just trying to help, but he hated being treated like an invalid. And what was worse was that no one else seemed to believe he was going to get better—that he was going to recover from this and get his life back. He knew he was—he could feel it. Why couldn't they?

"Ready to go, honey?" Mrs. Simmons called from the door, her hands poised delicately on the handles of the wheelchair.

"Sure," Will said. He decided to forget his usual protests and just let her come get him. It was easier that way. After all, if no one knew that he intended to beat this thing and get right back on the football field, no one would try to stop him.

"All right, Elizabeth," Mr. Nelson said, closing the thick manila folder that had her name on its cover. "It looks like you're pretty much on track with everything." He held the file upright and tapped it on his desk a few times, then placed it on top of the stack on the side of his desk.

Elizabeth nodded politely. "Okay, so then . . . am I

all set?" she asked, poised at the edge of her seat. If she got back to study hall now, she might have a shot at finishing her short story for creative-writing class.

"Actually, no," Mr. Nelson answered. He removed a new folder from his bottom desk drawer and began to thumb through it. "There is one other thing I wanted to talk about with you today, but it looks like I've run out of copies—I'll be right back."

Elizabeth sank back into her chair and glanced at her watch. *Ten-thirty.* There was no way she was going to get back to study hall in time. Mr. Quigley was going to kill her. This would be her third late assignment in the last week, and she knew he wasn't about to give her another extension. If only she could have finished the story last night. Unfortunately, ever since Conner had checked out of school and into rehab, Elizabeth hadn't been able to keep her mind on her writing.

Yeah, she and Conner had agreed to take a break from each other, but getting him out of her head hadn't been too easy.

After what seemed like forever, Mr. Nelson finally returned with a handful of photocopies. "Here you go," he said, handing a packet to Elizabeth. "Sorry that took so long—it seems like there's always a line for the copier around here," he said with a chuckle.

Oh, yeah, that's hysterical, Elizabeth thought, managing a weak smile as she glanced down at the papers he had handed her. Maybe she could fake a stomachache and go home early or something.

"So, as you can tell from the heading," Mr. Nelson began, gesturing to the handout, "the thing I wanted to discuss with you is the—"

"Lydia G. Senate scholarship," Elizabeth whispered. She glanced back up at Mr. Nelson, forgetting all about her short story. "Oh my God, I had no idea it was time for this," she babbled. "I mean . . . I know she announces the nominees at a different time every year so that no one can prepare for it in advance, but I kept thinking it would be later. Although I guess it's already pretty late in the year. Anyway, when's the deadline? What do I have to do?" She flipped through the pages, scanning for details.

"Well, actually, Elizabeth—," Mr. Nelson began.

"Um, Mr. Nelson?" she interrupted. "I think I'm missing a page." She frowned as she checked through the packet a second time. "I have all this stuff on the student judges and everything, but I don't see an application. Does that come separately from everything else, or do I need to—" Elizabeth stopped short. There was something in his expression—the angle of his head or maybe his slightly slack jaw—that made Elizabeth's chest tighten.

"What is it?" she asked. "Is there something wrong? I *was* nominated, wasn't I?" she added with a laugh. She shifted her legs, her gaze darting around the room. When she looked back at Mr. Nelson, he was staring at her intently, his lips pressed together in a thin line. "Wasn't I?" she repeated, her voice cracking.

Mr. Nelson exhaled slowly. "Well, actually . . . no," he said, squinting. "At least, not for the scholarship. But you were nominated to be on the board of student judges, which is also a great honor," he added quickly.

Elizabeth's shoulders slumped forward. "I . . . I don't understand," was all she could manage. She'd been waiting for this chance ever since she'd first heard about the Senate scholarship her junior year, and everyone else had always seemed to think she was a given for the award. How could she not even be nominated?

"I know you're disappointed, Elizabeth," Mr. Nelson said, "but as I'm sure you know, the requirements for this scholarship are very stringent, and unfortunately, even though you're an exceptional student, you just didn't make the final group."

"Why not?" Elizabeth asked, trying hard to speak past the lump in her throat. The corners of her eyes stung with tears that were on the verge of forming, and she blinked rapidly.

"Well, it's complicated," Mr. Nelson said. He folded his hands together, leaning forward. "Elizabeth, everyone here appreciates all your contributions to the school. However, many senior girls qualified for this scholarship, and the faculty was forced to nominate just five. It's possible that the decline in the quality of your work this fall was responsible for keeping you from making it into the final group. I really don't have all the information." He looked up at Elizabeth and shrugged. "I'm sure they had their reasons, though."

Elizabeth shook her head. She didn't want to cry like some toddler who hadn't gotten her way, but at the same time she couldn't believe she'd been passed over for this scholarship. Especially after she'd spent the last two years working toward it. All because she'd let her grades slip over a guy—a guy she wasn't even with anymore.

"I'm sorry, Elizabeth, but keep your chin up—there will be others."

Yeah, right, Elizabeth thought. *Keep your chin up. Hang in there.* As if it was that easy to get over something she'd been dreaming about for so long.

"And in any case, you have been selected as a student judge, so why don't I explain how that works?" Mr. Nelson continued.

"Oh, yeah . . . okay," Elizabeth said, biting her lip.

"All right. This is how it will go. I still have some photocopying to do, but by the end of the day today I'll get you a packet with your voting forms and information on each of the five nominees. That way you can take a look at all of the activities they've been involved with and any special honors or awards they've received in the last four years."

Elizabeth stared down at the papers in her lap. She swallowed, trying to focus on what he was saying, but it was like he was talking to her from the other end of a long tunnel—the words were hollow and muddled. She still couldn't believe she hadn't even rated a nomination.

"Then tomorrow, during periods five and six, you'll have a chance to interview the candidates to help you determine your vote. After the interview I'll ask that you and the other student judges stay through period seven to review the materials submitted by each of the nominees—teacher recommendations, brief essays, and the applications, which have a series of short-answer questions—and then I'll ask you to write your vote and turn it in by the end of homeroom on Friday morning." Mr. Nelson paused to take a deep breath. "So—does that all make sense? I know it sounds like a lot, and it's a pretty short deadline, but that's the way Mrs. Senate likes it. She says the faster the process goes—"

"—the less time the candidates have to improve their images," Elizabeth finished quietly, without looking up.

"Yes," Mr. Nelson said, knitting his brow and drawing back slightly. "Well, I—" He brought his hand to his mouth and coughed. "Excuse me. I guess that just about covers it. If you have any questions, you can feel free to stop in and talk to me again. Otherwise I'll get those forms to you this afternoon, and I'll see you at the panel tomorrow."

Elizabeth nodded, finally managing to look Mr.

Nelson in the eye again. "Okay," she said, standing and trying to look at least half dignified.

"Elizabeth—I am sorry you weren't nominated," Mr. Nelson said softly.

Elizabeth breathed deeply and nodded again. "Yeah. Thanks." And before Mr. Nelson could say anything else, she turned and rushed out.

As she walked toward the bathroom, she kept her eyes focused on the cool, beige tile floor, even though the hallway was basically deserted. And once she got there, the reflection in the mirror was exactly what she had expected—red-rimmed eyes and blurred mascara streaks.

"That's attractive," she muttered as she wiped her eyes with a tissue. She was definitely going to have to pull herself together—especially if she was going to sit through a group interview tomorrow and stare across a table at the five students who had beat her out without revealing just how devastated, bitter, and envious she was.

If I can pull that off, Elizabeth told herself, *maybe I'll qualify for an acting scholarship.*

"Did Coach Riley say anything about your amazing practice yesterday?"

Maria stiffened at the sound of the familiar voice ringing out above the buzz of noise in the hallway. She'd seen Melissa and Ken coming out of a classroom together as she walked past, but she hadn't thought they'd be able to keep up with her at her fast pace.

Maria tried to move even more quickly, but the halls were packed with between-class traffic. She searched the throng of students, hoping to see Elizabeth or Tia—someone to give her an excuse to stop or head the other way without looking like she was trying to avoid Ken and Melissa. But no luck.

Melissa's voice rang out over the crowd again, this time accompanied by a ridiculously exaggerated laugh. Whatever monosyllabic, Neanderthal comment Ken had managed, it had obviously amused Melissa.

"But you wouldn't have tackled *me,* would you?" Melissa asked coyly—or at least as coyly as she could while practically yelling out the words. "I mean, I *am* your girlfriend."

Maria shuddered. *That's it,* she thought, eyeing the girls' bathroom at the end of the hallway. It was definitely time for a hair and makeup spot check. *So Melissa will think she got to me—so what?* The girl was going to think whatever she wanted anyway. Maria was just about to duck out of the hall when she heard her name.

"Maria—can I talk with you for a moment?"

She turned to see Mr. Nelson standing by his office door, motioning to her. "Sure," she answered, eagerly crossing the hall. Saved by the guidance counselor—that was a first.

"What's up?" Maria asked, feeling her shoulders relax as soon as she was out of Melissa's direct line of fire. But Mr. Nelson hadn't heard her. He was looking at something off to her left.

"Melissa! Melissa Fox," he called, gesturing for her to join them. "This involves you too." Maria's jaw dropped. "I might as well kill two birds with one stone," Mr. Nelson added, smiling at Maria as Melissa approached. The tension that had left Maria's body seconds earlier resumed its grip.

"Why don't you ladies step into my office?" Mr. Nelson asked, waving his hand to direct them inside. Melissa nudged her way past Maria and followed him. *Well, excuse me,* Maria thought, glaring at the back of Melissa's head. Reluctantly she too made her way into Mr. Nelson's office, wondering what he could possibly have to talk to her about that involved Melissa. It wasn't like they had anything in common—a few classes and National Honor Society, but that was about it. They'd never served on any of the same committees or even worked together on a project. What could he possibly want to talk to both of them about? *Unless . . .*

Maria's heart stopped. *No way would he call us in here to talk about Ken,* she told herself. But it was the only thing that made sense. Maria had been kind of out of it ever since she and Ken had broken up—maybe Mr. Nelson had noticed and felt like he needed to do something about it. But that was ridiculous! Just who did Mr. Nelson think he was all of a sudden? The *dating* counselor?

Maria narrowed her eyes, watching as Mr. Nelson entered and closed the door behind himself. "What exactly is this about?" she asked. Her voice had a slightly harsh tone to it, but Maria didn't care. She wasn't about to sit down for some kind of girlfriend/ex-girlfriend mediation session.

"Having a bad day?" Melissa asked innocently. Maria scowled back at her, and Mr. Nelson blinked twice, looking back and forth between the two of them.

"Now, normally I'd speak to each of you separately about this matter," Mr. Nelson began, "but since you both had your scheduled appointments with me already before this came up, I thought I'd try flagging you down in the hall instead. And luckily I managed to get both of you at once."

Yeah, luckily, Maria thought.

"So anyway, the reason I called the two of you in here," he went on as he fumbled to pick up a folder from his desk. Maria took a deep breath and braced herself. "Ah—here it is," Mr. Nelson continued, handing each of them a packet of papers. "You've both been nominated to compete for the Lydia G. Senate scholarship."

"The . . . did—did you say—?" Maria stuttered. Her eyes widened with excitement as she scanned the front page of the handout. "The Senate scholarship!

Oh my God—this is *so* amazing." She beamed at Mr. Nelson and was almost reaching up to hug him when she heard a sigh.

"I'm sorry," Melissa interrupted, shaking her head, "but what exactly is the *Senate scholarship?*"

Maria's sudden euphoria vanished. For a second she'd forgotten Melissa was even in the room.

"The Senate scholarship is a prestigious award offered by one of our most distinguished alumni, Lydia G. Senate," Mr. Nelson began to explain. "It's a four-year scholarship to an East Coast school—Mrs. Senate has a list of options in the back of your packets—and each year it is awarded to a senior girl who meets all of the criteria set forth in the handout I've given you."

"Oh," Melissa said, raising her eyebrows. "Wow." She began flipping through the papers Mr. Nelson had given her. Maria clenched her jaw. What was Melissa doing in here anyway? It was enough to make Maria think that maybe a girlfriend/ex-girlfriend mediation session wasn't such a bad idea. At least it would be better than hearing that Melissa had been nominated for this scholarship—the one Maria had been dreaming of winning for almost two years now.

"So, like, how many people are competing for this?" Melissa asked, finally glancing up from her papers.

"Five," Maria answered before Mr. Nelson had a chance to speak. "And the winner is chosen through a combination of faculty recommendations, votes from the student board of judges, and a review of the candidates' applications, essays, and transcripts."

Mr. Nelson took a step back and smiled. "Well, Maria—it looks like you've done your homework," he said.

"Maria *always* does her homework," Melissa said in a sharp tone.

"Yes, well," Mr. Nelson said, once again furrowing his brow and looking back and forth between the two girls, as if trying to assess their relationship. *She's a vicious, manipulative boyfriend stealer,* Maria thought, smiling to conceal her bitterness. *Just in case you were wondering.*

"I don't want to make you girls too late for class," he said, grabbing a pad of pink late passes and beginning to fill one out. "So let me wrap things up. The biggest point to make is that this whole process happens very quickly. There are application materials due tomorrow afternoon, and the winner will be announced at a dinner on Friday night—so I'd encourage you to read these forms over completely and see me by the end of the day with any questions you might have."

"No problem," Melissa answered.

"I will," Maria said. Mr. Nelson nodded, then handed over the late slips he'd been scribbling for them.

At least AP English is just around the corner, Maria thought as she and Melissa filed out of the office together. But just before they reached the classroom door, Melissa stopped and faced her.

"So, are you looking forward to the competition?" Melissa asked with her usual smug smile.

Maria lifted her chin slightly and held Melissa's gaze. "Yeah, actually I am," she said.

Melissa let her eyes travel up and down Maria's body, taking in every inch of her jeans and sweater. "Yeah, I guess I would be too," she said slowly. "You know—if I had any."

Before Maria could respond, Melissa opened the classroom door and walked in, dropping the late pass on Mr. Collins's desk and taking her seat. Maria straightened her shoulders, then followed her into the room.

As if Melissa could even begin to compete with Maria when it came to something like a scholarship. This was one place where Melissa's cute little cheerleading uniform and conniving friends weren't going to help her. She was on Maria's turf now, and Maria was determined to win this thing and show the little snot who went after her boyfriend what losing felt like.

TIA RAMIREZ

LYDIA G. SENATE SCHOLARSHIP

<u>Application Form</u>

SECTION I: Short Answer

Write a brief (1–2 paragraphs) answer for each of the following four questions.

1. Why do you want to attend one of the prestigious institutions on the list?

THERE ARE MANY REASONS I WOULD LIKE TO ATTEND A PRESTIGIOUS EAST COAST INSTITUTION, THE MOST IMPORTANT OF WHICH IS . . . I'VE ALWAYS WANTED TO VISIT THE EAST COAST, ESPECIALLY NEW YORK CITY, AND . . . WELL, I'M NOT SURE, BUT ISN'T THERE USUALLY A REALLY GOOD BOY-TO-GIRL RATIO AT THOSE SCHOOLS?

SOMETHING TELLS ME THAT

WOULDN'T GO OVER VERY WELL WITH MRS. SENATE.

OKAY. TAKE TWO: THE BEST THING ABOUT ATTENDING A PRESTIGIOUS EAST COAST INSTITUTION WOULD BE . . . THAT IT WOULD LOOK REALLY IMPRESSIVE ON MY RÉSUMÉ SOMEDAY—NOT TO MENTION THAT A LOT OF THEM HAVE THOSE REALLY COOL SWEATSHIRTS WITH THE SCHOOL SLOGANS IN LATIN. I MEAN, WITH ONE OF THOSE I COULD GET A JOB ANYWHERE, RIGHT?

THIS IS PATHETIC. COME ON, TIA, THINK . . . THERE HAS TO BE AT LEAST ONE GOOD REASON I WANT TO GO TO AN EAST COAST SCHOOL . . . SOME REASON ASIDE FROM THE FACT THAT IT WOULD BE TOTALLY FREE IF I WON THIS SCHOLARSHIP. OH—OKAY, I'VE GOT IT:

THE MAIN REASON I WANT TO ATTEND A PRESTIGIOUS EAST COAST SCHOOL IS BECAUSE THE CAFETERIA FOOD IS BOUND TO BE BETTER. I MEAN, THEY CHARGE, LIKE, <u>TRIPLE</u> THE REGULAR RATE FOR ROOM AND BOARD, SO THERE MUST BE SOME SERIOUS COOKING GOING ON IN THE DINING HALLS, RIGHT? MAYBE EVEN A LITTLE TEX-MEX SO I WOULDN'T FEEL LIKE I WAS TOO FAR AWAY FROM HOME . . .

OKAY, SO THIS SUCKS. I'M JUST GOING TO MOVE ON TO #2 AND WORRY ABOUT THIS STUPID QUESTION LATER.

2. Which schools have you considered thus far?

UM . . . HELP?

CHAPTER 2
Conflict of Interest

"A full scholarship?" Ken asked, raising his eyebrows. He pulled a tray from the cart just inside the cafeteria door and passed it to Melissa, then grabbed one for himself.

"Thanks," Melissa said, holding the tray against her hip. "Yeah, it includes *everything*—room, board, tuition, books. She even pays for all the school supplies if you buy them at the campus store."

Ken let out a low whistle. "Sounds good."

"I know," Melissa said, shaking her dark, bouncy ponytail back and forth. "I can't believe I got nominated. And it happens so fast—I'll know if I've won by Friday." Suddenly Melissa took a step back and stared up at him, her eyes gleaming. "Do you realize that if I won, I wouldn't have to deal with loans or financial aid or any of that stuff?" she said. "I wouldn't even have to deal with guilt trips from my parents about how they were picking up the tab for everything. I could just pack up and get out of here without worrying about *anything*."

"Yeah, you'd have it made," Ken agreed. He

reached for a container of french fries just as Melissa plopped a small salad on her tray.

"We'd *both* have it made," Melissa corrected him as they inched forward, moving automatically with the rest of the line. "Don't forget your football scholarship."

She grinned up at him, and he smiled in return. He liked the way Melissa talked about his football scholarship as if it were a done deal. He'd never told her about what Mr. Krubowski, the Michigan scout, had told him that day in Coach Riley's office. How the football scholarship wasn't a sure thing until Ken proved he could take the pressure without quitting, the way he had in September. But seeing Melissa so confident helped Ken feel like it would all be fine. And it was also kind of cute the way Melissa seemed to think of them as a team even though they'd only been seeing each other for a couple of weeks.

"And I *know* I could convince Mrs. Senate to approve U Mich," Melissa went on, clutching Ken's upper arm. "I know it's not on her list, but it *is* a great school, and I heard she made an exception just a few years ago for someone who wanted to attend the Sorbonne in Paris."

"Michigan?" Ken asked, drawing back slightly. "I didn't know you were still thinking of . . ." Ken let his voice trail off. He knew Melissa had been planning to go to Michigan with *Will*, but he just assumed that plan had died along with their relationship.

"Well, yeah," Melissa said, the gleam fading from her light blue eyes. Ken shuffled forward, watching as Melissa gingerly lifted her tray and set it on the silver, metal bars of the cafeteria counter. She glanced over her shoulder at him, her eyes narrowed. "Does it bother you that I want to go to Michigan too?" she asked.

"No, no—not at all," Ken assured her, despite the sinking feeling in his stomach. "I was just kind of . . . surprised."

Melissa grabbed some plastic silverware from the bin and dropped it on her plate. "I *have* been looking at Michigan for a while, you know," she said, sounding almost defensive. "I mean, yeah, I only thought about it before because Will was going there, but now . . ." Melissa shrugged. "Now I want to go for me." She paused, holding Ken's gaze for a minute before continuing. "They have a great humanities program, and there are tons of museums and theaters around—it's supposed to be a really cultural area with a lot to do. Plus I checked out their campus online, and it looks really pretty."

Ken nodded. "Yeah, definitely—it looks like a really good school," he agreed, even though he didn't have a clue what the campus was like or even where in Michigan it actually was. But what else was he going to say?

"Plus it will be really good for us to be there together," Melissa added, choosing a roll from the bread basket. "I can support you in football since I'll still be cheering at all your games, and you can help me set up my apartment—there's no way I'm living on campus."

Ken winced—he couldn't possibly have heard her right. It was one thing for Melissa to follow Will to college—they'd been together forever. But for her to follow *him?* They'd barely been dating!

Ken watched as Melissa carefully opened a cooler door and pulled out a bottle of juice. "So . . . this scholarship," he started, hoping to get back to more comfortable ground. "How many other people were nominated?"

"Four," Melissa answered, plunking the juice down on her tray and holding the cooler open for Ken. "But Mr. Nelson couldn't say who they were—he hasn't talked to all of them yet. Although," Melissa said, one side of her mouth curving into a strange smile, "I do know who *one* of the other candidates is."

"Really? Who?" Ken asked. He grabbed a Coke, then put it back and took a carton of milk instead. Coach Riley kept reminding him to drink more milk.

"Your ex-girlfriend," Melissa said, her voice sharp. "As if she has a chance." She moved her tray to the last section of counter space and snagged an apple. Ken stared after her for a moment, a strange sense of pride filling his chest.

Way to go, Maria, he thought almost automatically. Then suddenly Melissa's comment hit him.

"What do you mean, 'as if she has a chance'?" he asked, catching up to her.

Melissa tilted her head. "I mean," she said, "I don't think she's got much of a shot." She held his gaze, staring back at him hard.

"How can you say that?" he asked, ignoring her expression. "Maria's practically the best student in this school—everyone knows she's going to be our valedictorian. And she's done a *ton* of stuff. School plays, student council, the newspaper—she's taken every AP course SVH has ever offered. Plus she . . ." Ken stopped, noticing that Melissa's features were tightening more each second, forming an intense glare. He gulped, realizing he'd gone a little overboard.

"Gee, Ken. I'm sorry if I insulted your ex," Melissa snapped. "I guess I didn't realize you were still so hung up on her."

Ken's jaw dropped. "What? . . . I'm not—," he started, but Melissa was already gone. He watched as she stalked over to the cash register, cutting in front of the rest of the students in line. A few girls gave her dirty looks, but no one asked her to move.

Meanwhile Ken remained where he was, paralyzed by Melissa's comment. Other students shuffled past, and the line moved around him, but his feet might as well have been glued to the ground.

Hung up on Maria? How stupid was that? Sometimes Melissa was so oversensitive, it was ridiculous. So Ken had stood up for Maria when Melissa insulted her—so what? Maria was a good person. And a good student. And she *did* have a shot at that scholarship.

Probably a better one than Melissa does, Ken thought—not that he would ever say it out loud. But it was true. And that was probably what was actually bothering Melissa.

He'd stuck his foot in his mouth, and now she was angry. All he had to do was sit back, stay neutral, and keep himself from mentioning Maria's name for the rest of the week. After all, the Senate scholarship didn't involve him, and the competition would be over by Friday night. Then Ken would be back on the football field, Melissa would be on the sidelines cheering for him, and everything would be back to normal.

"Okay, so now that you're both sitting down, I have some *incredible* news," Tia babbled, barely able to contain herself.

Maria pushed her cafeteria tray out of the way and leaned forward, resting her arms on the table. "What is it?" she asked, her dark eyes wide with curiosity. "You look totally pumped."

"Yeah, tell us already," Elizabeth prodded, even though she seemed more interested in removing the stringy pieces from her orange than in listening to anything Tia had to say. Something was bugging her, but whatever it was could wait until after she'd heard Tia's great news.

"Okay, but you're not going to believe it," Tia began. "I met with Mr. Nelson this morning—to go over college stuff, you know?—and he told me—are you ready?" Maria and Elizabeth both groaned in unison. "He told me that I was nominated for the Senate scholarship! Can you believe it?" Tia waited for her friends to explode into excitement with her, but instead they both just stared at her.

"Hel-*lo?*" Tia shook her head. "I'm not talking about some fifty-dollar scholarship here—this is the *Senate* scholarship," she repeated, "and I've been nominated! Isn't that great?"

"Yeah." Elizabeth nodded, avoiding Tia's gaze. "It is. Really." She split her orange in two, then glanced back up at Tia. "Congratulations."

"Yeah, congratulations, Tia," Maria echoed in an equally unenthusiastic tone.

Tia gaped at both of her friends. "Wow, you better be careful," she said. "I wouldn't want you to choke on all that excitement."

"I *said* congratulations," Elizabeth muttered, sliding her orange aside and focusing her attention on her salad instead. She speared a cherry tomato with her fork and shoved it into her mouth. Tia drew back and glanced at Maria, who just shrugged. She was obviously just as confused by Elizabeth's tone as Tia was.

"I *know* you said congratulations," Tia told Elizabeth. "You *both* did," she added, turning to Maria. "I guess I just thought you guys would be a little more excited for me, that's all."

"You're right. I'm sorry, Tia," Maria said, reaching across the table and touching her friend's arm. "I guess I was just a little caught off guard. See, there's something I have to tell you. Um, I was nominated too."

"You were? That's great!" Tia said. How exciting was that? Only five girls were nominated, and she and her friend had both made it.

"Thanks, Tee," Maria said, flashing a quick smile. "And I'm really sorry. I should have been that happy for you too. I guess I was just sort of surprised."

"Surprised?" Tia asked with a frown. "What—because I was nominated?" That couldn't be what Maria was saying. Could it?

"No, of course not," Maria said, blinking rapidly. "Not because you were nominated." She reached over to straighten her fork and spoon so that they were lined up neatly on her napkin. "I just meant that I'm surprised you would be interested in a scholarship with such, well, intense restrictions."

Tia pressed her lips together. What was Maria trying to say? She didn't think Tia could handle it? She glanced at Elizabeth, but Elizabeth seemed oblivious to the fact that there was a conversation going on at all—forget the fact that it involved her.

"I don't really understand what you mean," Tia said carefully, folding her arms together on the table.

"No, it's nothing," Maria said. She gave a short, nervous laugh. "I guess I just think of you as more of a going-out-and-partying kind of person, you know . . . not the hard-core academic type."

So, what, Maria didn't think Tia was smart enough to be nominated? Just because she didn't spend every free moment locked up in her room, studying?

"Look. I may not be a superbrain like you and Elizabeth," Tia said, "but I'm still a good student, and I've always been involved in lots of sports and activities—you don't even know half the stuff I did at El Carro. And I know you think that being captain of the cheerleading squad is no big deal, but—hello? Maria?"

Tia waved her hand to get Maria's attention, but Maria was fixated on something just off to the right. Tia glanced over to see Melissa and her friends Cherie and Gina sitting together at a nearby table.

Oh, great. Here we go again, Tia thought, watching the animation drain from Maria's face. Sometimes it almost seemed like Melissa had stolen Maria's personality along with her boyfriend.

"Sorry—what were you saying?" Maria asked, shaking her head.

Tia took a deep breath, trying not to get too frustrated. She knew how hard it was for Maria to see Melissa and think about her and Ken being together. "I was just saying that cheering is hard work, and the fact that I was made captain—"

"Okay, I know cheering's hard, and you're really good, and I know that I couldn't do one of those jumps to save my life, but—" Maria paused to shoot a glare at Melissa. "You have to admit," she continued, raising her voice, "some cheerleaders are just ego boosters for arrogant football players. Nothing but wanna-be athletes in short skirts and tight vests."

Tia's jaw went slack. Melissa didn't appear to have heard Maria, but Tia had gotten every word.

"Excuse me?" she demanded. "How can you say that to me?"

Maria started, shifting her focus from Melissa to Tia. The intensity of her friend's reaction had obviously caught her off guard. "I didn't mean *you,*" she muttered, rolling her eyes.

"Oh, really?" Tia asked through gritted teeth. She knew the comment had been meant for Melissa, but seriously—how could she not be insulted? "Are you sure? Because I wear the same short skirt and tight vest that Melissa does. Maybe I'm just a wanna-be athlete too."

Maria sighed. "God, Tia, don't take everything so personally."

"I'm not," Tia shot back. "But think about it—I

mean, first you act like it has to be some kind of freak accident that I got nominated for the Senate scholarship, and then you tell me cheerleading is just some kind of football fan club. How am I supposed to take that?"

"Why don't you guys give it a rest," Elizabeth interrupted. "You two are way too wound up about this scholarship. Let's just change the topic."

"Yeah, that's probably a good idea," Maria said. She gave Tia a weak smile.

"Whatever," Tia agreed. She tugged the red scrunchie off her wrist and pulled her hair into a loose ponytail. Suddenly it hit her that if she and Maria had been nominated, there was no way Elizabeth wouldn't be too. "So," she blurted out, turning to face Elizabeth. "Has Mr. Nelson talked to you about the scholarship yet?"

Elizabeth dropped her fork into her salad. "I thought we were changing the subject," she snapped.

Tia's eyes widened. "Sorry," she said, exchanging a confused glance with Maria.

"Well, Liz, he *did* talk to you, right?" Maria asked softly.

"Yeah," Elizabeth said, picking up her fork and poking at a piece of lettuce. "But I wasn't nominated."

"How could you *not* be nominated?" Tia asked.

"That can't be right. There has to be some kind of mistake," Maria protested.

Elizabeth just shook her head. "It's not a mistake. I wasn't nominated," she said. "Now—could we *please* stop talking about this stupid scholarship?"

"Sure," Maria said.

"Yeah, sure," Tia agreed. She stared into her mashed potatoes and began making trails with her fork. She knew Maria hadn't meant to insult her—she was just still raw from her breakup with Ken. And as much as Tia had hated hearing it, she had to admit Maria was at least partially right. Tia wasn't exactly thrilled about all the stiff requirements of the scholarship.

But still, it was such an amazing opportunity—four years at a good school, totally paid for. And Tia was just as capable of attending a tough East Coast school as Maria was—she wouldn't have been nominated for this scholarship if she wasn't.

And besides, this is my decision, Tia thought, starting to feel more confident. She wasn't about to let anyone else decide what was and wasn't right for her—especially when it came to something as important as where she was going to spend the next four years.

Ken yanked open his locker door, realizing that this was the first time he'd walked all the way from the cafeteria to here by himself since he'd started seeing Melissa. She usually walked with him to most of his classes too. But that probably wouldn't be happening for a while, judging from the death stare she'd given him in the cafeteria.

I wonder how long she'll stay mad, Ken thought, grabbing his physics text and the planning pad he used for woodworking class. He cradled his books in his right hand and ran his left through his thick, blond hair. A few curls fell onto his forehead, reminding him that it was time for a haircut.

Just play it cool until the end of the week, Ken reminded himself. By then the scholarship would be out of the way, and Melissa would calm down—she was just in crisis mode right now.

Ken eyed his reflection in the mirror Melissa had made him put in his locker last week. She had said he needed one too so she could check her makeup there if she didn't have time to go back to her locker between classes. *Definitely time for a haircut,* he decided, closing his locker door. He was just about to start down the stairs to the industrial-arts wing when he heard someone call his name. He turned to see Mr. Nelson coming toward him.

"Ken," Mr. Nelson repeated, clapping his hand on Ken's shoulder. "I'm glad I caught you—there's something I need to talk to you about. Let's step over here," he added, moving to a small alcove at the top of the stairwell.

Ken followed, his mind whirling. "What's up?" he asked, trying to keep his voice steady. There was only one thing this could be about: the football scholarship.

Maybe Hank Krubowski had contacted Mr. Nelson directly. . . .

"I have an exciting offer for you, Ken," Mr. Nelson said, pausing to look Ken in the eye.

"Yeah?" Ken responded, licking his lips. "What is it?" It was weird that Mr. Krubowski wouldn't have told Coach Riley first, but Ken didn't care—his dreams were coming true!

Mr. Nelson leaned forward, lowering his voice. "You've been selected to serve on the student board of judges for the Lydia G. Senate scholarship," he said.

Ken blinked, shook his head, then blinked again.

"Are you familiar with it?" Mr. Nelson asked, furrowing his brow.

"Um . . . sure," Ken sputtered, still wondering why he hadn't heard the words *football* or *Michigan* come out of Mr. Nelson's mouth.

"Well, then, you must know what an honor it is to be selected as a student judge for this competition. It will make a wonderful addition to your college applications."

"Yeah, I guess it will," Ken managed. Was that really all Mr. Nelson had wanted to talk to him about? What was the big deal about judging some stupid scholarship?

"Good, I'm glad you feel that way," Mr. Nelson said, thrusting a manila envelope into Ken's hands. "In this packet you'll find everything you need to act as a student judge—voting forms, Mrs. Senate's criteria for selecting a winner, and a schedule of events—the first of which is the panel interview tomorrow during periods five and six. I'll clear it with your teachers—you don't need to worry about it."

Ken stared down at the packet Mr. Nelson had given him and read the white label on the outside:

KEN MATTHEWS
STUDENT BOARD OF JUDGES
LYDIA G. SENATE SCHOLARSHIP

For the first time the name clicked in his brain.

"Wait—this is the *Senate* scholarship?" he asked, suddenly realizing what Mr. Nelson was asking him to do.

"Well, yes—that's what I said," Mr. Nelson replied, frowning.

"I can't vote on this," Ken said. He tried to hand the envelope back to Mr. Nelson, but he wouldn't take it.

"Of course you can," Mr. Nelson said. "You were selected by your teachers, which means they all think you'll make a very good judge. Besides, all the judges are students who head up activities representing the different aspects of student life at SVH. We can't exactly leave our *star quarterback* out, can we?" Mr. Nelson asked, chuckling as he patted Ken on the shoulder.

"No, you don't understand," Ken insisted. "I know two of the nominees pretty well—that's got to be some kind of conflict of interest or something."

"Ken, I'm sure *all* of the student judges know the nominees—that's why they're candidates," Mr. Nelson said. Ken cringed at the note of condescension in the guidance counselor's voice. "They're all student leaders who are very involved in student activities and therefore very well known," Mr. Nelson finished.

"But I know them *really* well," Ken protested. "One of them's my ex-girlfriend, and the other one—"

"I guess you'll just have to work twice as hard to be impartial, then," Mr. Nelson interrupted.

"But—"

"Read through that packet. I'll see you at the panel interview tomorrow," Mr. Nelson finished, turning to go.

Ken stared down at the manila envelope in his hands. "This sucks," he muttered, scuffing his sneakers against the tiled floor as he made his way to the stairwell. What was he supposed to do now? There was no way he could play it cool and stay neutral with Melissa for the rest of the week when he had to help pick a winner for this dumb scholarship. But the worst part was that now he really *did* have to choose between Melissa and Maria. And no matter who he voted for, he knew he was going to end up suffering for it.

* * *

Okay. So I got Mr. Collins to write a recommendation, now I just need to get— Maria stopped dead when she entered the auditorium. She had intended to ask Ms. Delaney to be her other faculty reference for the Senate scholarship, but Tia was already engaged in a lively conversation with their drama teacher. *She'd better not be doing what I think she's doing.*

Maria walked closer to the stage and stopped about three feet away from Tia and Ms. Delaney, waiting until they finished talking.

"Thanks so much," she heard Tia say as she backed away from Ms. Delaney, a ridiculous smile stretching across her face. Then she turned abruptly and jogged over to sit in the front row, next to Jessica.

"Excuse me, Ms. Delaney?" Maria said.

Ms. Delaney turned quickly, the fringe on her dark emerald scarf fluttering against her black dress. "Maria," she said with a smile. "What can I do for you?"

Maria stood up straight and tried to sound as confident and calm as Ms. Delaney always did. "I wanted to ask you to write a recommendation for me—for the Senate scholarship."

"Oh." Ms. Delaney's smile stiffened, and Maria felt her stomach sink. "I'd love to, but I'm afraid I can't," she said.

Maria glanced past Ms. Delaney at Tia, who was

laughing about something with Jessica. "Why not?" she asked, a bad taste in her mouth.

"I just finished telling Tia I'd write one for her," Ms. Delaney explained. "And I simply don't have time to write another one tonight—I'm swamped with college recommendations as it is. I'm sorry, Maria, but I can't do it. I'm sure you'll be able to find someone else," she finished.

"Yeah, sure," Maria said. "Thanks anyway." Reluctantly she plodded over and plunked herself down on the other side of Jessica.

"Hey—I heard you got nominated for that Senate-scholarship thing," Jessica said. "Congratulations."

"Thanks," Maria said, without much enthusiasm. She sat back in her seat and folded her arms across her chest. How could Tia have done that? Everyone knew drama was Maria's big thing—couldn't Tia have asked someone else?

"Are you okay, Maria?" Jessica asked, crinkling her nose slightly.

"I'm fine," Maria said. "I'm just kind of bummed that Ms. Delaney can't write a reference for me," she added.

"Oh, no," Tia said, cupping her hand over her mouth. "It's not because she's writing mine, is it?"

Duh, Maria thought. "Actually, yeah, I think it is. She said she doesn't have time to write two of them right now."

Tia winced. "I'm sorry, Maria. If I'd known you

were planning to ask her, I would have held off."

Well, you know now, Maria thought, waiting for Tia to offer to find someone else. But Tia didn't say anything. Where did this girl get off?

"That's okay," Maria finally said. "I can find someone else. In fact," she continued, "I was thinking of asking Coach Laufeld."

"Coach *Laufeld?* The *cheerleading* coach?" Jessica asked.

Maria nodded, flicking a piece of fuzz off her pants.

"But you're not a cheerleader," Tia argued, clearly upset.

Yeah? Well, five lines in a play don't exactly make you an actress, but that didn't stop you from getting a reference from Ms. Delaney, did it?

"I know," Maria said. "But I've had her for gym class for three out of four years. She might be a good reference to show I'm well-rounded. My transcript already shows what I can do in academics."

Tia shifted in her seat. "Well, yeah," she said, reaching up to readjust her ponytail, twisting the scrunchie tighter. "But . . . well, I sort of thought Coach Laufeld might be a good reference for *me.* You know, because of cheering and everything. I mean, she *did* make me captain."

"Oh, you're right," Maria pretended to realize. "I can't believe I didn't think of that," she lied. "Of course she'd be a good reference for you—go ahead and ask her. I'm sure I can find someone else."

Jessica's face twitched, and Maria was pretty sure she was on to her, but Tia let out a relieved sigh, apparently clueless.

"Thanks, Maria," she said. "I really appreciate it."

"No problem," Maria responded. *Now it's your turn.*

"And I'm sure you're right—it will be easy for you to find someone else," Tia went on. "I mean, I'm sure just about any teacher in the school would write one for you."

Okay, so either Tia's been cheering so long that she's actually turning into a ditz, or I'm the most incredibly convincing actress that ever lived, Maria thought. Not that it mattered. Either way, she wasn't getting the recommendation from Ms. Delaney. As if it wasn't bad enough that Tia was competing for a scholarship she didn't even want—now she was doing it with *Maria's* reference.

Lydia G. Senate Scholarship
Student Board of Judges Ballot

Please indicate which candidate you are voting for by making an *X* next to her name. Then in the space provided please write a brief paragraph explaining your vote. You should base your vote on the listing of candidates' activities and class rankings, the group-panel interview, the candidates' essays and applications, and how well each of the candidates demonstrates leadership, scholarship, and a commitment to maintaining excellence while attending an approved postsecondary school.

_____ Leah Castellana
_____ Melissa Fox
_____ Hannah Galloway
_____ Tia Ramirez
_____ Maria Slater

I have voted for Elizabeth Wakefield because:

Dear Mrs. Senate—

I was not nominated for this scholarship, but I would like to take this opportunity to explain to you why I think I deserve to be the recipient of your generous award anyway.

Okay, so it's kind of a lame idea, but it could work. I could declare myself an independent and launch a write-in campaign. Maybe Mrs. Senate would be impressed. In fact, maybe she'd admire my initiative so much, she'd forget about the other nominees and give the scholarship to me.

Yeah, right.

CHAPTER 3
Runner-up

"Good meeting, Maria," Steve Anderson said as they walked out of Ms. Gilbert's room on Wednesday afternoon.

"Thanks," Maria said, trying to hide a chuckle. He'd said those same three words to her following every student-council meeting since the beginning of the year, regardless of how things had actually gone. Steve claimed it was part of being a good VP—always being ready to pump up the president's ego—and it had become sort of a joke between the two of them.

The two of them had been on student council together since freshman year, so even though they'd never had a lot of classes together, they'd still gotten to know each other pretty well. And this year they were working together more closely than ever since Steve was vice president and Maria was president.

Maria glanced over at him as they walked down the hallway, noticing that he was one of the few guys at SVH who was actually taller than she was, even when she was wearing heels. She peered more closely at his jet-black hair and sharply angled jawline. Why had she never noticed how cute Steve had gotten this year?

Probably because of Ken, Maria thought. After all, back when she'd *had* a boyfriend, she hadn't exactly spent a lot of time looking at other guys. Although if she'd known Ken was going to ditch her for Melissa, maybe she would have.

They had just turned the corner when Steve stopped suddenly and faced her. "Hey—do you have any plans right now?" he asked, his voice cracking slightly. "I mean, do you want to grab a cup of coffee or something?"

Maria felt her eyes widen. Was Steve asking her out? "Um, sure," she started, totally caught off guard. "I mean, no—I can't, sorry." She bit her lip, wishing she could have just said yes and gone with him.

"Oh," Steve mumbled. "Okay." He turned to go, but Maria stopped him.

"Maybe some other time," she offered. After all, Ken had moved on, so why shouldn't she? Besides, Steve was a great guy, and it would do Ken good to see her with someone new. It would probably do her some good too. "It's just that I have to run down to the *Oracle* office, and then I need to get home and start working on my application for the Senate scholarship," she explained.

"The *Senate* scholarship?" Steve echoed, arching his eyebrows.

Maria squinted. "Yeah—why?"

A wide smile stretched across Steve's face. "Mr. Nelson snagged me right before student council to tell me I'm on the board of student judges," he said.

"You're kidding!" she exclaimed.

Steve shook his head. "But I didn't know you were one of the nominees—I haven't had a chance to look at my packet yet," he said, holding up a sealed manila envelope.

"Wow—that's really funny," Maria said, eyeing the envelope. She was dying to ask him to open it so she could see who the other two nominees were.

"Yeah," Steve agreed, shuffling his feet. "Well . . ."

"Well," Maria echoed. "I guess I'd better get going," she said.

"Yeah, me too," Steve said. "So I'll see you at the group-panel interview tomorrow." Maria nodded. "And maybe we'll get coffee some other time?"

"Yeah, definitely," she agreed, before turning to walk down the hall to the *Oracle* office.

This was really turning into a great day. First the Senate scholarship, and now a potential date with a cute guy. If it hadn't been for the fact that Tia and Melissa were nominated too, things would have been just about perfect.

Maybe my slump is almost over, Maria thought, reaching for the door to the *Oracle* office. It was cracked open, and she was just about to push it all the way when she heard something that made her stop.

"What I don't get is why Mr. Collins is writing a recommendation for Maria and not you." Maria recognized the voice right away. It was Tina Ayala, a junior who worked as a staff photographer for the *Oracle.*

"What do you mean?"

Elizabeth.

Maria flattened her body against the wall and stood just outside the door, listening.

"Well," Tina continued. "I went to see Mr. Collins after fourth period today to show him some pictures I had of the last girls' soccer game, and Maria was in there, talking to him."

"So?" Elizabeth responded.

"So, she was asking him to write her a recommendation for the Senate scholarship, and I was just kind of surprised. I mean, you're the *Oracle* editor, and you've been writing for the paper forever, so I just assumed he'd be doing one for you. Weren't you mad that she asked him first?"

Maria shook her head. She'd been writing for the *Oracle* for a long time too, and she had Mr. Collins for AP English. She deserved his recommendation just as much as Elizabeth did. Why would Tina be so rude?

"I might be, if I'd been nominated," Elizabeth answered. There was more than a hint of bitterness in her tone. Wow—she was taking this pretty hard. Maria would have too, though.

"You weren't nominated?" Tina asked.

"No. In fact, I'm actually on the student board of judges."

Maria gasped, then clapped her hand over her mouth, hoping they hadn't heard her. So *that's* why Elizabeth had been so freaked out about the whole scholarship thing at lunch. It wasn't just that she hadn't been nominated—it was that she knew she'd have to choose between Maria and Tia.

Poor Liz, Maria thought. She'd be pretty upset if she were in that position.

"The student board of judges?" Tina echoed. "That's ridiculous. You should have been nominated—everyone at SVH knows you're the best student in the senior class!" Maria narrowed her eyes. She was going to remember this the next time Tina asked her for help with one of her assignments.

"I wouldn't go that far," Elizabeth said.

Modest as ever, Maria thought with a smile.

"Oh, please, of course you are," Tina insisted. "You deserve that scholarship more than anyone else."

Maria felt her blood pressure beginning to rise. She felt like bursting in and setting Tina straight, but then they'd know she'd been eavesdropping. Besides, she was sure Elizabeth would do it for her.

Come on, Liz, stand up for me.

The room was quiet for a moment. "So, what are you working on now?" Elizabeth finally asked.

Maria held back a scream. Why did everyone

keep treating her like a runner-up? First Ken dumped her for Melissa, and now Elizabeth couldn't even tell Tina that she deserved the scholarship as much as Elizabeth did. Meanwhile Tia was running around stealing her references.

That's it, Maria thought, turning to stalk back to her locker. Forget the *Oracle*—she was going home to work on her scholarship application. And when it was time for the group-panel interview tomorrow, she was going to kick some butt.

I'm going to get this scholarship no matter what everyone else thinks, she told herself. Now more than ever, Maria needed to prove to everyone—Ken, Melissa, Elizabeth, and especially herself—that she could come in first for once.

"Nice," Jade muttered to herself as she noticed the silver Mercedes parked in front of her apartment building. "Must be lost," she decided, pulling her Nissan to a stop next to the fancy car. People with rides like that tended not to live in her neighborhood.

She stepped out of her car and gave the Mercedes a closer look. It reminded her of Jeremy's, except that it was obviously much newer. Jade whistled as she hefted her backpack from the passenger seat.

Practice had been especially excruciating that afternoon—and not just because of the workout. It had been doubly exhausting because she'd had to listen to Jessica babble nonstop about Jeremy and how thankful she was that Jade had helped them get back together. As if Jade really wanted to hear happy-couple stories about her ex-boyfriend so soon after they'd broken up.

Whatever, Jade thought as she walked through the courtyard of the apartment complex. It didn't matter now anyway. Practice was over, and more than anything Jade was looking forward to just flopping down on the couch and vegging out for a while.

But as she approached the door to her apartment, she noticed a man standing in front of it. His back was to her, and she saw him raise his wrist to check the time on his watch, then shake his head.

She frowned, not sure what to do. The guy was dressed in what looked like a really expensive suit—he obviously wasn't trying to break in or anything. Did bill collectors make home visits?

She took another step closer, and then the man turned around. She gasped when she saw his face.

"Dad?"

Even though she hadn't seen him for years, the old mixture of fear and tension wrapped around her instantly.

"Jade." He nodded, a slight smile appearing on his round face. Slight. "It's good to see you." He stepped forward and held out his arms. Jade stared awkwardly for a moment, feeling like she had just walked into some kind of time warp, then moved closer, accepting a brief hug.

"What . . . what are you doing here?" she asked, squinting with confusion. "Shouldn't you be in Oregon?"

Mr. Wu laughed in his usual rigid way, as if one of his business clients had just made a weak joke. "Is that any way to greet your father?" he asked.

Well, yeah, considering I haven't spoken with you face-to-face since I was thirteen.

"Actually, I'm in town on business," Mr. Wu continued. "It was kind of a last-minute trip, and I figured since I was going to be so close to Sweet Valley, I might as well stop in and pay you a visit."

"Oh," Jade responded, still trying to process the fact that her father was even there.

"I tried to call last night," Mr. Wu explained, "but I couldn't get through."

Jade nodded slowly. "I was probably on-line," she offered. She tried to think of something to say, but her mind was blank. What was she supposed to talk to him about anyway? The weather?

"Shall we go inside?" Mr. Wu asked, gesturing toward the door. "After all, I've been waiting for a half hour now."

"Oh, sure," Jade said, fumbling for her key. She pushed it into the lock and began to turn it, suddenly remembering just what the apartment looked like inside. "Um," she began, turning back to her father, "the place is kind of . . . messy," she finished, swallowing hard.

"I'm sure it's not too bad," Mr. Wu said.

Jade cringed, remembering how immaculate her father had always insisted they keep their house when she was younger—before he and her mom had gotten divorced. As far as she could recall, he had never lifted a finger himself. Cleaning was supposed to be all her mom's job, with help from Jade. And if one piece of furniture was slightly out of place, Mr. Wu would lose it.

Jade entered the apartment first, closely followed by her father, who stepped gingerly—probably afraid of what his precious Armani shoes would come in contact with. Jade took the second to survey the living room. Laundry—clean but unfolded—was piled up on a chair near the door, spilling onto the crumb-laden blue carpet. Jade's books and papers were strewn across the floor by the coffee table. A glance through the open doorway into the kitchen told her what she'd already known. Dirty dishes were stacked up in the sink, and old newspapers and junk mail littered the table. All in all, she didn't think it was too bad—cluttered, but not really *unclean.*

She turned to catch her father's reaction and saw the disgust in his eyes.

"Does it always look like this?" he asked.

Jade pressed her lips together. "Of course not," she lied. She crossed over to the center of the room and started stacking her books together in one pile. "We've just been really busy," she said, glancing up at her dad.

"I see," Mr. Wu said. He traced a line in the dust on the bookshelf with his finger, and his frown deepened.

"I've had cheering practice every day and tons of homework, and Mom's been working a lot too—it's not easy being a single parent, you know," she added, letting her voice rise slightly.

"I realize that, Jade," Mr. Wu said evenly.

"Right." She nodded. "So anyway, we just haven't had a lot of spare time to clean lately. We were going to tackle it together this weekend."

Mr. Wu's gaze slowly traveled around the room, and then he turned to peer into the kitchen.

"Well, I need to get back to my hotel for a dinner meeting," Mr. Wu said. "I expected to find you here, doing your homework. I didn't realize you would be coming home so late."

Why did everything he said always sound like some kind of angry accusation? How was she supposed to know he would be there waiting?

He reached in his pocket to pull out his car keys, and Jade eyed the familiar Mercedes symbol on his key ring.

"That's *your* car out there?" she asked.

The corner of her father's mouth curved upward in a more genuine smile than she'd seen so far. "The

Mercedes? Yes, but it's a rental. I asked for a newer model—like the one I drive at home—but I'm afraid that was the best the agency could do."

"Oh, too bad," Jade replied, trying to hide her sarcasm. Leave it to her father to flaunt his material success even as he refused to pay a cent of child support unless Jade was holding down a steady job, since he knew her mom didn't have the resources to go after him in court. "Well, sorry we won't get to spend more time together, then," she said.

"Actually," Mr. Wu began, fingering his key ring. "I don't leave until Saturday. I was hoping we could have dinner Friday night. Just the two of us."

Jade flipped through a mental list of excuses. "Um . . . I don't know—I might have to work late." There was no way he could argue with that after all his big speeches about jobs and responsibilities, blah, blah, blah. . . .

"Perhaps you could reschedule," her father said. "It's not every day that your father comes to town—I'm sure your boss would understand. If you'd like, I'd be happy to give him a call."

"No, you don't need to give *her* a call," Jade said. The last thing she needed was her father sticking his nose into her workplace too. It didn't look like she was getting out of this. "I can probably switch shifts with someone else," she said. She couldn't bear the thought of sitting through an entire meal with him, but at least if she got through that night, maybe he'd get over the messy apartment and then just go back to Oregon for another four years.

"Good. I'll give you a call tomorrow night to confirm," Mr. Wu said.

"Okay," Jade said. "So, you'd better get back to your meeting or whatever."

"Yes, right," Mr. Wu said. His eyes darted around nervously, like he wasn't sure where to look. "I'll see you on Friday, then."

"Yep," Jade agreed. She breathed a deep sigh of relief the second he was out of the apartment, then shut and locked the door. She leaned back against it, closing her eyes.

First she had lost Jeremy, the only decent guy she'd ever gone out with, and now she had to deal with dinner with her dad. At least things couldn't get any worse.

"*Aie,* late again," Tia mumbled to herself, fumbling to unlock her front door. It was the second time that week she'd gotten home after dinner had already started—her parents were going to kill her.

"You're late, Tia," her mother said as Tia rushed into the kitchen and took her seat. Tomás and Miguel, Tia's youngest brothers, stared into their plates and tried not to giggle, but fourteen-year-old Jesse didn't even try to hide his amusement.

"What's your excuse this time?" Jesse demanded, smirking at his sister.

"*Sea silencioso*, Jesse," Mr. Ramirez scolded him. Jesse glanced sheepishly from his sister to his father.

"Well, Tia?" her mother prompted.

"I'm sorry. I know I'm late—but I have really good news," Tia said. If she could distract them with the scholarship, maybe she wouldn't have to tell them she'd been hanging out at the mall with Jessica and Andy for the past hour and a half. "I was nominated for a scholarship today," she announced proudly.

Mrs. Ramirez cocked her head. "A scholarship? That's wonderful—what kind of scholarship?"

Score! Tia thought, noticing that her father was also leaning forward with interest.

"Actually, a great one," Tia replied. "It's a full scholarship—all four years paid—tuition, room and board, books, supplies . . . everything. And only *five* senior girls can be nominated for it."

"Tia! That's wonderful!" her mother cried. She looked over at her husband. "Isn't it wonderful?"

"Yes, of course." He turned to Tia. "Congratulations," he said with a smile. Tia could tell he was proud of her, even though he was more reserved than her mother.

"Thanks," Tia said. She reached for the bright yellow serving bowl—nearly empty now that her brothers had finished with it—and began scooping the mixture of rice and pinto beans onto her plate.

"So you say you've been nominated—what

happens now? How is the winner determined?" Mrs. Ramirez asked. She pushed her plate forward and clasped her hands neatly on the edge of the table.

Tia rolled her eyes. "Actually, I have a ton of stuff I need to turn in for it, but I've already gotten my faculty recommendations—from Ms. Delaney and Coach Laufeld—so now I just have the application, which is a bunch of short-answer questions, and an essay to write," she said. She replaced the serving spoon and set the bowl back in the center of the table.

"Can I be excused?" Tomás asked, slumping down in his seat.

"Not yet," Mrs. Ramirez said firmly. "We're having a family conversation."

"But I'm done eating," Tomás protested. "And I'm bored."

Mrs. Ramirez sighed and glanced at her husband, who shrugged. "All right," Tia's mother continued, glancing at Tomás's plate. "Two more bites of your enchilada and you may go."

Tomás seized his fork and quickly plunged two pieces into his mouth. He looked up at their mom with a wide grin. "Done," he pronounced.

Mrs. Ramirez cracked a smile. "Okay, go on," she said.

Tomás hopped down from his seat and made a run for the living room.

"Can I go too?" Miguel asked.

"Me too?" Jesse added.

Mr. and Mrs. Ramirez exchanged tired glances as Mrs. Ramirez waved her two remaining sons away. "But no TV until you've finished your homework," she called after them.

Tia giggled as she served herself an enchilada from the clear-glass casserole dish. "This looks great, Dad," she said.

"Thanks," Mr. Ramirez replied. "Now, tell us more about this scholarship."

"Well," Tia started, quickly swallowing a bite of her enchilada. "It's paid for by this woman named Lydia Senate, who I guess graduated from SVH, like, a long time ago, and it's really strict. I have to write my essay and fill out my whole application tonight so I can turn them in tomorrow, and then there's this panel interview thing during fifth and sixth periods where student judges will ask us all kinds of questions."

"And you just found out about it today?" Mrs. Ramirez asked, her eyebrows shooting up.

"Yeah—that's what I mean," Tia said. "I guess Mrs. Senate likes to have it all happen fast so she can see the students for what we are, without lots of time to prepare." She shrugged. "In a way, I'm kind of glad it's going so quickly—at least I won't have to wonder whether or not I'm going to get it for a long time. They're announcing the winner at a dinner at Mrs. Senate's house on Friday night—you guys are invited to that."

"That *is* fast." Mrs. Ramirez shook her head.

"But obviously we're thrilled for you, Tia," she added. "It really is quite an accomplishment, whatever happens."

"Thanks," Tia said with a grin. "I'm pretty excited too. Although I'm not sure about going to an East Coast school."

Both of her parents jerked up in their chairs.

"A what?" her father demanded, his tone suddenly serious.

"You aren't really thinking about moving across the country, are you?" Mrs. Ramirez asked. "You don't want to do that."

"Well . . . no. I mean—" Tia glanced back and forth from her mother to her father. "I *wasn't,* but that's one of the conditions of the scholarship."

"Conditions?" Mr. Ramirez repeated. "What other *conditions* are there?"

Tia looked down at her plate, moving the rice around with her fork. She hated hearing that note of disgust in his voice. He was obviously already against the whole thing.

"Well, I guess the big one is that the winner is supposed to attend one of the approved schools on Mrs. Senate's list," she began. "There are a lot to choose from, and they're all really good schools—like Harvard, Brown, Bowdoin, Smith," she said, trying to remember other names from the packet. "There's a whole list if you want to see it," she offered.

"But they're all on the East Coast?" her mother asked.

"Well . . . yeah." She paused. "Look," she continued, "I haven't made any decisions yet. I may not even get the scholarship."

"But what if you do?" Mrs. Ramirez asked.

"Then I'll have four years of school paid for at a great college," Tia said. She dropped her fork with a loud clang. "Shouldn't you be *happy* about that?"

"I don't think we should talk about this any more tonight," Mrs. Ramirez said. She stood and started piling the dishes together.

Tia glanced at her father, hoping for support. But he just sighed, then got up to help his wife.

"I'm filling out the application," Tia snapped.

"Fine," her mother said, banging the plates together as she set them down next to the sink.

"And I'm going to the interview tomorrow too," Tia added. Neither of her parents responded. She shoved the rest of her enchilada in her mouth, then stood and walked out of the kitchen.

What's wrong with everyone? she wondered as she headed down the hall to her bedroom. Why couldn't her parents just be happy for her? Especially since having her college education totally paid for would relieve a huge burden for all of them.

Tia flopped down on her bed and buried her head in her pillow. Okay, so going all the way across the country wasn't exactly what she'd had in mind, but that didn't mean everyone had to completely shoot it down. If that was the way they were going to react every time she had an opportunity to do something new, maybe it *was* time Tia got out of her parents' house. Maybe moving three thousand miles away from her family wasn't such a bad idea.

Jade Wu

Photography: Ms. Murray

A good picture captures more than just people or things—it captures a mood, tells a story. Comb through your old family albums and select three pictures that you think accomplish this task. For each picture write a brief description of the action and explain what kind of mood or what story you think has been captured by the image.

Photo #1:

Description: My parents' wedding day—supposedly the happiest day of their lives. My mother is throwing the bouquet while my father watches.

Mood/Story: This picture definitely captures a mood—the mood of my parents' entire marriage. It shows my mother throwing back her head and laughing while the sleeve of her dress slips off her shoulder. All the people around her are smiling and laughing too—except for my father. He's standing in the background, staring at her bare shoulder and scowling. If someone had shown my mom that picture before the wedding, it might have saved her from making the biggest mistake of her life.

Photo #2:

Description: Me in my ballet shoes and tutu when I was six years old. I look like I'm twirling around because my hair is pretty long, and it's sticking straight out, and I'm holding my hands together above my head. My mom is squatting down, smiling and clapping, and my father is reading the newspaper. I know it's him because I can see his bald spot over the top of the paper.

Mood/Story: Typical day in my family. Mom's going all out to get involved in whatever I'm doing, and

Dad's probably checking to see how the stock market did that day. He probably doesn't even realize we're in the room.

Photo #3:
Description: Me in a white cap and gown, graduating from eighth grade. I'm holding up my diploma, and I'm standing with my mom. I remember that day. My favorite teacher, Ms. Heinrich, took the picture.
Mood/Story: My dad wasn't there.

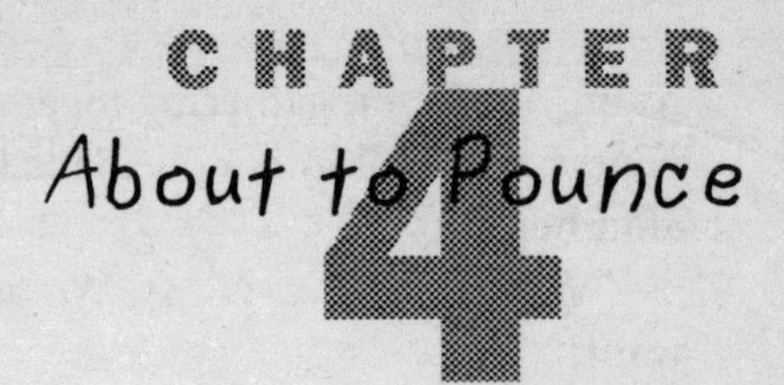

CHAPTER 4
About to Pounce

Jade watched as her mother placed the bowl she'd just washed onto the dish-drying rack, humming to herself. She licked her lips and decided that she had to quit stalling. She'd been trying to work up the nerve to drop her bombshell ever since they'd finished their late dinner.

"Um, Mom?" she said, her voice cracking. "I almost forgot to tell you . . . Dad stopped by this afternoon."

Ms. Wu froze. "Your father?" she asked. "He was . . . here?" She turned and scanned the kitchen, her eyes filling with concern. She wiped her wet hands on a dish towel, then took a step closer to Jade. "I don't understand—why did he come?"

"He said he was in town for business," Jade explained. She followed her mother's gaze to the mess outside in the living room. "But he was only here for a minute," she added. "And I told him how busy we've both been. He didn't seem to notice how . . . out of place everything was," she lied.

Ms. Wu nodded, then headed out into the living

room. She began gathering together all the old newspapers and mail into a pile. Jade bit her lip, then ran after her.

"What did he say?" Ms. Wu asked. "What did he want?"

Jade shrugged. "I'm not sure," she said. She hated seeing her mother like this—tense and nervous, mortified at the thought of her ex-husband seeing the apartment messy.

"Mom, it's okay," she said, trying to prevent her mother from beginning an all-out cleaning frenzy. Ms. Wu was clearly exhausted from working all day at the bank after a late shift at the bar last night. If she didn't stop rushing around like this, she was going to end up in the hospital again.

"Really," Jade insisted, catching her mother's arm before she could begin folding laundry. "I don't think he even noticed the apartment. He wasn't here long; he just came by to—" Jade stopped short. No way was she going to tell her mom she was having dinner with him on Friday night. Ms. Wu would spend the rest of the week trying to clean up the apartment to impress him. It was like she thought she had to prove something to him. *Besides,* Jade thought, *Mom has to work Friday night—she won't even be around.* And what she didn't know couldn't hurt her. "He just came by to say hi," she finished.

"That seems odd," her mother said. "Why would

he stop by like that—just out of the blue—and then leave so suddenly? It doesn't make sense."

"I don't know," Jade said. "He's flying back to Oregon tonight," she lied.

Ms. Wu stopped. "He is?" she asked, her face relaxing slightly. Jade nodded. "So, then, he just came all the way out here to say hello? That really doesn't sound like him."

"I don't know," Jade said. She reached over to straighten the sofa cushion, avoiding her mother's gaze. She didn't like lying straight to her face. "He was probably hoping you'd be here so he could flaunt his rental car—it was a Mercedes. *Not anywhere near as nice as the one he drives at home,*" Jade added, trying to imitate her dad's snobby tone.

Ms. Wu laughed. "That sounds about right," she said. "So—how did he look?"

Jade shrugged. "Same as ever," she said.

Ms. Wu nodded, a glint of pain in her eyes—the same glint that always came when the subject of Jade's dad came up. And he seemed to have walked away from his wife and daughter without a second thought. It just wasn't fair.

Ms. Wu sank down onto the sofa. "We'll tackle this place on Saturday, then," she told Jade with a grin.

Jade breathed a sigh of relief. *Saturday,* she thought. By then her father would be safely back in Oregon and out of her life—where he belonged.

* * *

Maybe I should finish my history homework first, Ken thought, replacing the receiver in its cradle for the fourth time in the last hour. He'd been putting off calling Melissa all night, but he knew he was going to have to do it sooner or later. Ken inhaled deeply, then forced himself to punch in Melissa's number.

After three rings he almost hung up, but before he could bail, he was greeted by Melissa's lukewarm, "Hello?"

Ken sucked in his breath. She already sounded annoyed, and she didn't even know it was him. "Um, hi—Melissa?" He hesitated. "It's . . . Ken."

"I *know* who it is," Melissa said. "So what's wrong? Did you remember something amazing about Maria that you forgot to tell me this afternoon?"

Ken's eyes widened. The girl could get vicious when she was mad.

"No, actually," he said. He was beginning to wonder if he'd made a mistake. But if he didn't tell Melissa he was one of the judges for the Senate scholarship up front, she was going to be even angrier than she already was.

He cleared his throat. "I just wanted to tell you that Mr. Nelson caught up with me in the hall right after lunch, and . . ."

"And what?" Melissa demanded.

Part of him just wanted to hang up on her—why

should he put up with this? But he reminded himself that she was just stressed about the scholarship. After all, things had been fine between them until this had come up. And she was being so supportive and encouraging about his football scholarship. She probably just wanted him to do the same for her—but instead he'd talked about how much *Maria* deserved it. He could kind of see why she'd gone off on him.

"Okay," Ken said. "It's just that . . . well—I'm one of the student judges for that scholarship you were talking about."

Silence, Ken thought. *This could be a good sign.* Maybe Melissa realized what a tough position he was in. Maybe she was thinking how cool it was of him to call and tell her about it even after she had avoided him all afternoon. She might even be feeling a little guilty.

"I just wanted to let you know before the group interview tomorrow and everything," Ken added.

"So I guess you've got a choice to make," Melissa finally replied. "You know what? We probably shouldn't even be talking right now. I mean, I'm a candidate, and you're a judge—isn't that a conflict of interest or something?"

Ken groaned. "Melissa—," he started, but before he could protest, there was a loud click in his ear.

Ken stared at the white receiver in his hand, shaking his head. Maybe things had gone as far as they were going to go with Melissa. Sure, she was supportive and everything, but sometimes it just didn't seem worth it. It was so hard to figure out where she was coming from or what she wanted from him—although he had learned one thing tonight: Silence from Melissa was definitely *not* a good sign. It simply meant that she was about to pounce.

Here we go again, Elizabeth thought as her sister barged into her room. She focused more intently on her computer screen, hoping that Jessica would take the hint and leave her alone.

"What are you working on?" Jessica asked, doing a belly flop onto Elizabeth's bed.

"History homework," Elizabeth said without moving her gaze.

"Jeremy's really good at history, you know," Jessica started. "He's in AP."

Another conversation about Jeremy. Why am I not surprised? Elizabeth thought.

"Maybe you guys could study together sometime or something," Jessica continued. "I think he's even considering majoring in history in college."

"That's great for Jeremy," Elizabeth replied through clenched teeth.

Jessica swung her legs around and sat up. "What's with you?" she asked.

"What do you mean, what's with me? Just because I don't feel like hearing more warm, cuddly

Jeremy stories doesn't mean something's *with* me," Elizabeth snapped.

Jessica let out an indignant sigh. "Touchy much?" she said.

Elizabeth ran her hand through her hair, then gave her temples a quick rub. "Some of us just have work to do," she said.

"Fine," Jessica said. She jumped up and started to walk out. "But you know what? You've been really uptight lately, and it's getting old."

"Excuse me?" Elizabeth said. She finally turned away from the computer to face her sister.

"I'm serious, Liz. This is your *senior* year, and for a while there I really thought you were starting to lighten up, but now you're even more wound than you used to be."

"Well, good," Elizabeth said.

Jessica's eyebrows shot up. *"Good?"*

"Yeah, good," Elizabeth repeated. "It's about time I got back on track. Do you realize the only reason I wasn't nominated for the Senate scholarship is because I let my grades drop this year? And do you know why? Because I've been totally caught up in Conner." Just thinking about how stupid she'd been made Elizabeth even more angry at herself. "I've been rearranging my life around him and for what? Now he's gone, and there's this huge gaping hole, and everything I spent the last three years working for is slipping away from me."

"It's just a scholarship, Liz," Jessica said quietly.

Elizabeth almost laughed. Leave it to her twin to miss the picture entirely. "A *full* scholarship, Jess," she said. "One I've been working toward for over *two years.* And I didn't even get *nominated.* Do you know how that makes me feel? Now I don't have Conner, and I don't have anything else either. You know, this was supposed to be *my* year. I broke up with Todd, but look what I did—I gave up everything for a guy again. And now I don't even have the guy!"

Jessica blinked. "I didn't realize you were so upset," she said. "I'm . . . sorry."

Elizabeth felt a twinge of guilt for laying this all on her twin. It wasn't Jessica's fault she'd messed up her life. "Yeah, well," she said, staring down at her hands and flicking the wine-colored nail polish off her index finger.

"At least you got nominated to be a judge," Jessica offered. "That's something, right?"

Elizabeth snorted. "Yeah, it's *something.* And it's going to be really something tomorrow at the group interview—when Tia and Maria realize I'm on the board, and I have to choose which one of them to vote for."

Instant Messages

jess1: So what's up at your house tonight?

jaames: The usual. Trisha's trying to read over my shoulder, and Emma's begging Mom to go out for ice cream. You?

jess1: Liz is totally stressed, my mom and dad are already in bed, and I'm talking to the cutest guy I ever met.

jaames: Anyone I know?

jess1: Very funny.

jaames: Wow. Funny and cute. You might have to hold on to that guy, whoever he is.

jess1: Ha ha. So do you have any plans for the weekend?

jaames: I was hoping to hang out with the hottest girl I know. Maybe you can bring the cutest guy you ever met, and we can double date.

jess1: Sounds like a plan. Where should we take them?

jaames: Anywhere but House of Java.

jess1: Yeah, I'm not really up for a group scene. I'd like to get that cute guy alone.

jaames: Watch what you write—Trisha's still

spying—but I know what you mean.

jess1: Hi, Trisha!

jaames: She says hi, but she still says she's not trying to read what we're writing.

jess1: That's okay. I have to go anyway. I'll call you tomorrow night, and we can figure out what we're doing. With our dates, I mean.

jaames: I'll be waiting by the phone.

jess1: You better be. Bye!

jaames: Bye.

[one minute later]

jess1: Why aren't you logging off?

jaames: I was waiting for you.

jess1: Oh.

jaames: So go ahead.

jess1: You go ahead.

jaames: You first.

jess1: How about if we both do it at the same time?

jaames: Okay. 1 . . . 2 . . . 3! Good night.

jess1: Good night!

CHAPTER 5
Staying Neutral

Tia hugged her books to her chest as she hurried out of English class. Her heart was pounding so hard, she felt like it was about to burst free and fly down the hallway on its own. She'd been on edge about the group interview all morning, and now that the time had actually come, she was a total wreck.

"Hey, Tee—wait up," a familiar voice called from behind her.

Tia turned to see Maria rushing down the hall. She looked perfectly put together in her long, pressed black pants and silky button-down shirt. Tia glanced down at her cargo pants. Was she supposed to dress up for this thing?

"Hey, Maria," she said, flashing a smile. As soon as Maria caught up, they fell into step together and headed toward the conference room where the interviews were being held.

"So," Tia started, quickening her pace to match Maria's. "Are you ready for this?"

"Yeah, sure," Maria said with a shrug. She didn't seem at all nervous. "I mean, it's not like we're taking a test or anything. We just have to answer a few questions." *Yeah, I guess,* Tia thought, feeling a little better. When Maria put it that way, it didn't seem like such a big deal. After all, an interview was really just a kind of formal conversation. And making conversation was definitely one of Tia's strong points.

"Besides," Maria continued, "I doubt they'll come up with anything I haven't already answered in one of my mock-college interviews or on another scholarship application somewhere."

Mock interviews? Tia thought. *Other scholarships?* Her heart started racing again. *That's it. I'm dead.* She hadn't even chosen which schools to apply to, and here was Maria—having *mock interviews.*

"I wish I could be that relaxed," Tia said. "I can't stop obsessing about what kind of stuff they might ask me. I've even been trying to figure out who the student judges are, but nobody seems to know. It's like this is some kind of big secret and—"

"Elizabeth is a student judge," Maria interrupted.

Tia stopped. "Elizabeth *Wakefield?*"

"Yeah," Maria replied. "Come on, we have to hurry up."

Tia started walking again, but she couldn't get why Maria was acting like this was no big deal.

Poor Liz. There was no way she would want to be in that position—Tia wasn't even sure she liked being in the position *she* was in. Still—why hadn't

Elizabeth told her? She'd obviously said something to Maria—how else would Maria have found out?

Elizabeth probably just didn't get a chance to tell me yet, Tia told herself. The way this scholarship was moving, Elizabeth might not even have known herself until this morning. Tia had to stop second guessing her friends.

Then again, Elizabeth and Maria are both super-competitive about school. It was something Tia had never understood—how people could get so worked up over GPAs and class rankings. She cast a sidelong glance at Maria as they neared the conference room. Maria's tight, serious expression made it seem more like they were going into battle than a scholarship interview.

Then again, maybe that's what this is for her, Tia thought. *A battle.* And with Elizabeth on the board of judges, it was a battle for more than just a scholarship. They were competing for Elizabeth's vote, which made it seem kind of like they were fighting for her friendship too.

"Ken, I believe you have the next question," Mr. Nelson said.

"Oh, yeah." Ken glanced down at his notes for one that hadn't been asked yet. In his packet of judging forms he had received a list of sample questions to use for the group-panel interview, although students were encouraged to come up with their own.

Between finishing his regular homework and working up the nerve to call Melissa, Ken had only managed to make up two questions, and of course they had been the first two asked.

Number eight, he thought, scanning the list. *This looks good.* Ken cleared his throat. "Um, okay. How would you handle the pressure of maintaining a GPA of 3.5 or better while participating in a minimum of six activities at a highly competitive school?"

Mr. Nelson nodded approvingly at Ken, then turned his gaze to the panel. "Hannah, you're first this time," he said. Ken watched as Hannah Galloway, a plump girl with black hair and dark, deep-set eyes, straightened herself in her seat and folded her hands on the table in front of her. She took a deep breath.

"During high school," she began, "I've worked really hard to keep my grades up while participating in a lot of activities, and I believe I could do the same in college by staying focused on my goals. I'm also an extremely organized person, which helps me to keep on top of all of my work, and I'm really good at spreading out my assignments over time—I'm not a procrastinator."

Ken nodded and smiled when she finished, then turned to Mr. Nelson, unsure what else he was supposed to do.

"Leah?" Mr. Nelson prompted.

Leah Castellana pushed a strand of long, straight brown hair behind her ear. "Um, I think I could handle the pressure because . . . I've done really well with it in high school, and getting all my homework done has never been a problem for me even when I have a late track meet or something."

Ken tried to make eye contact with her as she spoke, but she never looked up except to gaze off to the side of the room, as if that's where the student judges were actually sitting. He noticed Steve Anderson, the VP of student council, jotting something down on his notepad.

"Tia?" Mr. Nelson said.

Tia leaned forward slightly and squinted, biting her lower lip. She seemed much more relaxed than she had been at the beginning. When they'd started, she had been totally rigid. Now she was sitting almost casually—her elbows resting naturally on the table.

"Well," she started, looking directly at Ken. "I guess one thing I'd do to make sure I didn't get too stressed out would be to hang out with my friends and go dancing or something." She paused for a minute to flip her long, dark hair back over her shoulders. "I mean, I think good grades are important and everything, and I'd try really hard to do well in all my classes, but when it comes right down to it, friends are more important because sometimes going out and having a good time is the only thing that will keep you sane." She paused, flashing a quick smile. "Oh—and I plan to still do cheerleading and volleyball in college because I think sports really help you to unwind and handle stress a lot better too," she added.

"Thank you, Tia," Mr. Nelson said. "Melissa?"

Ken stiffened as Melissa stared into his eyes, realizing this was not only the closest he'd been to her all day, but also the first time she'd made eye contact with him since the interview had started. He'd glanced at her a few times, but she was still giving him the cold shoulder. Now, however, she was smiling at him—although he guessed it was a forced smile put on for the benefit of Mr. Nelson and the other judges.

"Good question," she said, her voice smooth, as if she were being interviewed by someone on the *Today Show* rather than the boyfriend she'd been ignoring for the last twenty-four hours.

She moistened her lips and straightened her posture. "Like Tia said, I'm planning to do sports in college too, and I think that will help me deal with a lot of the stress," she began. "I really enjoy being active, and I always feel better after a good workout at cheering or going for a run. And I also liked what Hannah said about doing well in high school and how that will help in college. I've kept my grades up, and I've been involved in a lot of activities too, so I don't think it will be hard for me to do the same thing in college."

Ken smiled at Melissa when she had finished, but she appeared to be looking straight through him. *Fine,* Ken thought. *Whatever.* If that was the way she was going to be, he might as well stop trying too.

"And last but not least, Maria," Mr. Nelson said.

"Thanks." Maria smiled at him, then turned to the judges, finally focusing on Ken. She met his gaze directly without flinching. "I think everyone else brought up some important points," she said. "I know the work habits I've established in high school will help me out a lot when I get to college, and I agree with Tia that balancing out all the work with some play is a good idea. But the two things that will really help me to be successful in college are my determination and my family. My determination because whatever I do, I always give it my all. And my family because they encourage me and they keep me grounded. And I know that even when I'm way across the country, my mom and dad, and even my sister, Nina," she added with a chuckle, "will always be behind me one hundred percent."

There was silence when Maria finished speaking, and Ken noticed Steve Anderson scribbling madly on one side of him and Abbi Richardson, the yearbook editor, writing just as furiously on the other. Maria turned to give each of them one last smile, but her gaze lingered a little longer on Steve. Ken glanced at Steve and noticed that he was grinning just as widely back at her. What was that about?

Ken shifted uncomfortably in his chair, aware of a strange, hollow feeling in his chest. Was there something going on between Maria and Steve Anderson?

That's impossible. It wasn't like they even knew each other that well, right? Maria had never talked about him or anything.

Ken glanced back at Maria just in time to see her blink and look away from Steve, her expression suddenly shy.

Shy? he thought. *Maria?* Ken scowled at the thought of Maria seeing someone else so soon after they had just broken up. Sure, he was with Melissa, but that was different. Melissa had just sort of been . . . there.

Ken sighed. He let himself shoot one more glance toward Maria, taking in her long, graceful neck. He'd almost forgotten how beautiful she was.

He caught himself staring at her and forced himself to focus on his notepad instead, but then, for some reason, his eyes were drawn to the right.

Oh, great. Melissa was giving him a serious death glare. She must have noticed him watching Maria. Now she was really going to think he was hung up on his ex.

So much for staying neutral.

If I can just get through the rest of this without a major slipup, I'll have a really good shot at winning.

Maria smiled to herself and not just because of the way Steve had been grinning at her throughout the interview. After that last question about handling the pressure of school, she knew she was doing well.

"Okay," Mr. Nelson said, studying his clipboard. "Elizabeth—it's your question."

Maria watched as Elizabeth edged forward in her seat, her face blank. Maria hadn't seen her smile yet. It was obvious that she didn't want to be there—at least not as a judge—and Maria couldn't help feeling bad for her. Still, she couldn't forget the way Elizabeth had totally skipped the chance to stick up for her with Tina yesterday.

"Elizabeth?" Mr. Nelson prompted.

Elizabeth nodded, then glanced down at the papers in front of her. "What college do you hope to attend, and what subject do you want to major in?" she asked. Her voice was a dull monotone, and Maria wondered if she'd even been paying attention to any of the other questions and answers.

"Maria—you can answer first this time," Mr. Nelson said, nodding at her.

"Thank you," Maria said, smiling, but when she turned back to Elizabeth, she found it hard not to grit her teeth. She reached for the glass of water to her right, stalling for time. She knew she couldn't let her resentment seep into her answer—better to just give Elizabeth a quick grin and focus on Steve instead.

"Excuse me," Maria said, after taking a few sips of water. "I've actually been working on an early acceptance application to Yale, which I plan to send in by the end of the month, and that's my first choice. But I'm also planning to submit applications to Dartmouth and Princeton. As for my major, I intend to focus on political science with a minor in African American studies, and then pursue a law degree concentrating on civil-rights litigation."

When Maria finished, Steve flashed the same gorgeous smile he'd been giving her every time she answered a question, and Maria felt her face glow. He was the first guy who'd looked at her that way since she and Ken had started dating, and it felt good.

"Thank you, Maria. Leah—you're next," Mr. Nelson said.

Leah nodded, and Maria noticed that her hands were shaking even as she tried to hide them under the table. But at least this time she actually looked up. "I've submitted an application to Brown for early decision, and I had an interview there last week that went really well," she said.

What? She'd had her interview? Maria hadn't realized she should already be at that point.

"But like Maria," Leah continued, "I'm submitting applications to Princeton and Dartmouth, even though Brown would be my first choice." Maria couldn't help noticing that Leah's voice was beginning to sound more confident, even if it was still a little shaky. Maybe she just needed some time to warm up. "And I'm going to be a biology major on the premed track because I'm planning to be a heart surgeon someday."

Heart surgeon, Maria thought. *Great. That beats civil-rights lawyer.*

"Thank you, Leah," Mr. Nelson said, grinning. *Well, of course* he's *impressed,* Maria thought bitterly. Leah was ahead of schedule—she'd filled out forms. It was enough to impress any guidance counselor. "Hannah—let's hear from you," Mr. Nelson said, consulting his notes.

Maria watched closely while Hannah folded her hands calmly on the table, just as she had before each answer. "Well, it looks like Maria, Leah, and I might end up at the same school," she said with a light laugh. "I've also submitted an early decision application to Harvard and one to Princeton—where my mother and father both went," Hannah continued, smiling at Leah, who smiled back sincerely. Maria had to restrain herself from rolling her eyes. She felt like reminding them that this was a competition—they weren't sorority sisters yet. "And I'm planning to send applications to Yale and Georgetown as well, just in case."

Oh, great, Maria thought. *My first choice is her safety school.* She could hardly wait to hear what Hannah's major would be. Was it possible to major in sainthood?

"And my major," Hannah went on, "will be a double one—international relations and public policy."

All right, so she's not going for sainthood. She's going for president. Somehow that didn't make Maria feel much better. She was beginning to realize that as good as some of her answers had been, she had some real competition in Hannah and Leah. They were both excellent students, incredibly involved in school and community, and they were way ahead of her in terms of applying for colleges. But it wasn't just that—it was *where* they were applying. Harvard and Brown—those were Mrs. Senate's alma maters. Maria bit her lip and wondered if it was too late to change her answer.

"Thank you, Hannah," Mr. Nelson said. "Melissa—your turn."

"Well," Melissa started, "I've been looking at the University of Michigan for a long time, although I realize it's not on Mrs. Senate's list."

Not on the list? Maria thought. *Hello? It's not even on the East Coast!*

"But still," Melissa continued, "I think it would be a great school for me. They have a really good humanities program, and it's a culturally rich area with a lot of museums, theaters, and libraries. I'm certain I could get Mrs. Senate to approve it. Although if she didn't, of course I'd be willing to look at some other schools."

Maria's mouth fell open. Who did this girl think she was? Then she glanced around at the student judges, amazed to see them nodding like they actually bought what Melissa was saying. Was Maria the only one who thought Melissa should be eliminated right away for being geographically challenged?

"Thank you, Melissa," Mr. Nelson said. "And finally, Tia."

Maria couldn't help cringing as she prepared herself for the crazy answer that would come out of her friend's mouth this time. Even though she was still annoyed at the way Tia had stolen Ms. Delaney's recommendation away, she felt bad that the girl was making such a fool of herself. Handling school stress by partying all night? Please.

"Actually, I haven't really decided on a college yet, but I have been looking at UC Berkeley and UCLA, which both seem really cool," Tia began. "But of course, like Melissa said, if I won the scholarship, I'd definitely be willing to look at some schools on the list. I haven't picked a major yet either. I guess I just kind of thought I'd figure it out on the way. I mean, who really knows for sure what they want to do ten years down the road anyway?"

The judges and a few of the nominees laughed, but Maria couldn't believe it. Tia had gone way too far. Did she think this was just a game? It seemed obvious that she wasn't serious about the scholarship. Tia clearly wasn't looking for the kind of intense college experience that Mrs. Senate had in mind, so why was she even bothering? It didn't make sense. As far as Maria was concerned, Tia should have disqualified herself at the start. Then at least the scholarship would go to someone who actually intended to use it.

Melissa Fox

Dear Ken,

I saw you staring at Maria all through the interview—you were practically drooling. So I guess I was right, wasn't I? You're still hung up on her. How cute. Well, let me tell you this—I'm not going to hang around just to be your backup girlfriend. I hope you have fun visiting her at Yale. Just don't count on her coming out to Michigan for any of your football games.

—Melissa

Okay, so I'm never going to give him this note. But I will say it to him if I have to.

CHAPTER 6
PAINFULLY SERIOUS

"And when I mentioned Jeremy, she practically bit my head off," Jessica said, leaning back against the brick wall of the school.

Too bad she missed, Jade thought, taking a bite of her turkey sandwich.

She and Jessica were eating lunch outside in the courtyard together—Jessica to avoid her stressed-out friends and Jade to get some fresh air and keep from getting too worked up about having dinner with her dad. But so far, it wasn't working. Between listening to Jessica rant about her friends and rave about Jeremy, Jade was beginning to think dinner with her father would be a welcome relief.

"I mean, I can kind of understand how Liz would be disappointed about not being nominated and everything," Jessica continued. "But it's beyond that. The three of them are so crazy that I can't even stand being in the same room with them. You'd think something bigger than a scholarship was on the line."

"It almost makes me glad my grades aren't good

enough to get nominated for all that stuff," Jade said. "Although a free ride to college wouldn't be bad," she added. With that kind of money behind her, she'd never have to deal with her father again.

"Yeah," Jessica agreed. "I'll just be glad when Friday's over."

"Me too," Jade said under her breath.

"What's happening Friday?" a deep voice asked.

Jade glanced up to see a tall, lean figure standing over them. She couldn't see his face very well through the glare of the sun—but she could make out the dark, straggly hair hanging down close to his shoulders.

"Evan," Jessica said, shielding her eyes with her hand as she squinted up at him.

"Hey, Jess," he replied. "What's up? Why are you so anxious to have Friday over?" He squatted down next to Jessica, and Jade was finally able to get a good look at him. His skin was tanned to a light brown, and he had a little stubble on his face. Cute, but nothing special.

Jessica shook her head. "It's this Senate-scholarship thing—have you heard about it?"

"Oh, yeah," Evan said with a nod. "Leah mentioned it to me at swim practice yesterday—she was really psyched about it. I didn't know you were nominated, though," he added.

Jessica blew a puff of air at her forehead, causing a few stray blond hairs to flutter. "Yeah, right," she said. "I think you know me better than that."

Evan turned to Jade for an explanation, and for the first time she noticed his piercing blue eyes. Her breath caught in her throat. He did a good job of hiding it, but this Evan guy was seriously good-looking.

"Um," she started, swallowing hard. "It's not the scholarship that's stressing Jessica out—it's her friends," she managed. Luckily Evan turned back to Jessica, giving Jade a chance to breathe.

"See—Maria and Tia were nominated," Jessica explained, "and they're at each other's throats. And Liz *wasn't* nominated for the scholarship, so she's all bent about that, but she *was* chosen to be one of the judges, so she has to vote for Tia or Maria or one of the other candidates, which just makes things worse." Jessica exhaled heavily, and Evan shook his head.

"Sounds rough," he said. He flicked his gaze back over to Jade.

"I'm Jade, by the way," she said, finally regaining control of herself. Not many guys could cause a reaction like that in her.

"Hey, Jade, nice to meet you," he replied. "I'm Evan." He smiled, and Jade noticed that despite all the scruff on his face and his somewhat rugged appearance, Evan had perfectly straight, gleaming white teeth.

"Sorry," Jessica said with a shrug. "I'm lame with introductions."

"Only with introductions?" Evan teased. Jessica lightly socked him on his shoulder, drawing Jade's eyes to his well-toned arms.

He laughed, then started to stand up. "I've got to get going," he said. "Good luck with that scholarship stuff," he told Jessica. "And Jade—it was nice to meet you. Maybe I'll see you around somewhere," he added before ambling off across the grass.

"Okay, so what's the scoop on him?" Jade asked as soon as he was out of earshot.

"The scoop?" Jessica repeated, narrowing her eyes. "His name's Evan Plummer, he's on the swim team, and he's a really nice guy."

"Yeah, yeah," Jade said, waving her hand, "but how do *you* know him?"

"Oh," Jessica said, biting her lip. "Well, I kind of met him through Liz—he's a friend of Conner's, really, and I *almost* dated him for a little while, but we decided we made better friends."

Great, Jade thought. *The second-cutest guy I've ever seen, and he's wrapped around Jessica's finger too.*

"Then things got kind of weird for a while," Jessica continued, "because he sort of started to see Liz, and they almost got together, but that didn't work out either."

"That is kind of weird—*almost* dating identical twins," Jade agreed. She stuffed a potato chip in her mouth and waited for Jessica to finish another bite of her sandwich, trying to let enough time pass so that her next question wouldn't be too obvious. "So—is he seeing anyone now?" she asked.

"I don't think so," Jessica said, "but you know, I'm not really sure. I guess I'm just so happy with Jeremy, I don't really care who anyone else is dating."

Jade looked down at the ground. Sometimes Jessica had no clue what she was saying. But she wasn't supposed to be hurt by that, right?

"Oh, I'm sorry," Jessica said. "I didn't mean to—"

"Hey—it's all right," Jade cut her off. "I mean, I helped you guys get back together. I'm fine with it, really."

It wasn't a total lie. She'd get over Jeremy soon. Especially with guys like Evan Plummer around and—hopefully—available.

"Jessica, Tia, and Maria, you'll be the fourth group," Ms. Delaney said, gesturing for the three of them to move to the last remaining corner of the stage.

This should be fun, Tia thought, joining Maria and Jessica. Maria hadn't spoken one word to Tia as they walked from the conference room to drama class. In fact, she hadn't even looked at Tia since midway through the group-panel interview. *She's probably just upset because she didn't do so well with the last few questions,* Tia thought.

While everyone else seemed to have loosened up toward the end of the interview, Maria had remained painfully serious—as if her life depended on every last word she spoke. Even Leah, who had been beyond shy in the beginning, had lightened up by the time it was over.

"Now, in your groups," Ms. Delaney continued, "I want you to take the prop I've placed in your corner and create a meaningful dialogue around it. We'll rejoin in ten minutes." Then she clapped twice, and the room began to buzz.

Tia leaned forward and picked up the plastic, jeweled crown she, Jessica, and Maria had to work with. "I think you should wear it, Jess," she said, setting it on Jessica's head with a grin.

Jessica turned her nose to the ceiling. "It does suit me, doesn't it?" she joked.

"Well, you are a *princess,*" Tia offered, smirking.

"Ha ha," Jessica said. She removed the crown and handed it back to Tia. Out of the corner of her eye Tia could see Maria standing stiffly, her arms folded across her chest. *Oo-kay,* she thought. *I guess we won't be getting any help from the drama queen today.*

"Oh—I have an idea," Jessica blurted out. "What if we pretend that there's a queen who's missing, and all we've been able to find is her crown?"

"That's good," Tia said. She squinted at the ceiling for a moment, then stood up straight, both feet together. "The queen is missing," she announced in an exaggerated English accent as she held the crown up high.

Jessica broke into laughter. "Who are you supposed to be?" she asked between giggles.

"I'm the village crier," Tia said with a frown. Jessica always laughed at her characters.

"More like the village idiot," Jessica teased. Tia scowled at her.

"Well, if you're the village crier, what are you doing with the queen's crown?" Maria asked, her arms still folded.

It's a miracle—she can speak! Tia thought. "I don't know—maybe I found it in the street," she said.

Maria shifted her arms to her hips. "I think maybe you stole it," she said. Tia's jaw practically dropped at her tone.

"Oh, that's really good," Jessica said, ignoring the obvious resentment behind Maria's statement. "We'll make Tia the thief, and maybe—"

"But why would I steal the crown?" Tia asked. "It's a *crown*. It's not like I could walk down the street and pawn it at Ye Olde Pawne Shoppe."

"I don't know," Maria said with a shrug, her eyes still trained on Tia. "It doesn't really make sense. It's kind of like going after a scholarship you don't even want."

Tia groaned. So that was her problem. "What makes you think I don't want it?" she demanded, placing the crown back in the box with the other props.

"Hello—Berkeley? It's not exactly an East Coast school."

"You heard Melissa," Tia shot back. "Mrs. Senate

has made exceptions before—and besides, I said if I won, I'd look at other schools."

"Um, guys?" Jessica said. "I think we're getting off track. Let's—"

"Oh, yeah, Melissa—there's a reliable source," Maria scoffed. "And just which schools would you look at anyway? You don't even know what you want to major in—you said it yourself during the interview."

"Look, just because I don't have the rest of my life planned out the way you do—"

"I'm not talking about the rest of your life. I'm talking about the next four years," Maria said. "The Senate scholarship is supposed to go to someone who's *serious* about college—not someone who wants to hang out at Berkeley, taking classes in the art of Ultimate Frisbee and partying with her friends."

Tia exhaled sharply and shook her head. "Is that what you think I'm going to do?" she asked.

"I don't know," Maria admitted. "But I don't think you have a clue what you want to do either." The volume of her voice had decreased, but the hostility was still there. The worst part, though, was that Tia knew Maria was right. She *didn't* know what she wanted to do in college—she didn't even know where she wanted to go.

"Okay—so anyway, about this crown," Jessica tried again, but neither Maria nor Tia shifted their gaze.

"I deserve this scholarship just as much as you do," Tia said, clenching her hands into fists at her sides.

"But do you even *want* it?" Maria asked. "Because I don't think you do."

Why did everyone keep trying to tell her what she wanted? Maria was so sure she didn't want to go to a good school, and her parents were convinced she didn't want to travel to the East Coast. When did Tia get to decide what Tia wanted?

"Let's just do the skit," Tia mumbled. She grabbed the crown and placed it on her head. "But I'm not going to be the thief," she added. Because she wasn't *stealing* anything. She was only going after something that she'd earned as much of a right to as anyone else—including Maria—had.

Finally, Maria thought when the bell rang at the end of drama class. She bolted up the ramp to the back of the auditorium and out the door. Once she reached the hallway, she took a deep breath. At least she had put some distance between herself and Tia, but she still couldn't calm down. What if Tia won—then what? She'd probably go to NYU for a semester and end up transferring back to California—then *no one* would get to use the Senate scholarship.

Maria sighed and tried to practice some of the breathing exercises they'd been working on in drama class. She definitely needed to chill out. But just as she rounded the corner, she saw the one person who could upset her even more than her fight with Tia had.

Ken was heading right toward her. *Where's Barbie?* she wondered, trying to avoid making eye contact.

"Hey—Maria."

She stopped. The sound of his voice saying her name affected her in a way she never would have predicted—and definitely didn't like. What did he want with her?

"I was kind of hoping I'd run into you," he said, inching closer.

She tried to unfreeze her muscles and move to the side of the hallway, but it wasn't happening. "What for?" she asked. It was the first time he'd even spoken to her since the night they broke up.

"I just wanted to tell you that I thought you were really good—you know, during the whole panel thing," he said, waving his hand back in the direction of the conference room. "And also . . . I wanted to say good luck."

"Good luck?" she echoed, unable to comprehend what was going on. Ken Matthews, Mr. It Guy, was standing here talking to her like they were on friendly terms or something. Like he hadn't ditched her for a cheerleader the second he'd become popular again.

"Look, Ken, I don't need your pity, and I don't

need your luck," she told him, once she'd remembered she could speak. "And most of all, I don't need you pretending to be my friend. So you can just go on and cast your vote for your manipulative little girlfriend and leave me out of it." As the words tumbled out of her, she felt all the pain of their breakup hitting her again, as fresh as the moment he'd turned and walked away from her front door. "As far as I'm concerned, your vote is worthless anyway," she blurted out. "The only reason you got elected to the board of judges is because football is so overrated around here. And let's face it—if this had happened a couple of weeks ago, Will Simmons would be judging, wouldn't he?"

Before she could fully take in his shocked expression, Maria pushed her way around him and took off down the hallway. If her pulse had been high after fighting with Tia, now it was off the charts. At least there were only forty-five minutes left in the school day, then she could go home and collapse.

Forty-five minutes, Maria thought, willing herself to keep walking. Because if she stopped for even one second, she wasn't going to be able to wait until she got home. She was going to collapse right now.

Ken Matthews

I have voted for ~~Maria Slater~~ because:

~~I know Maria works really hard and cares a lot about school, and I'm sure she'd do the same in college. She's also a good student leader, a great actress, and someone who's really serious about making a difference in the world.~~ Forget that—I left out how judgmental she is and how she can't ever cut anyone a break. Plus she thinks all football players are automatically jerks, and she's kind of snobby and stuck on herself too.

I guess I almost forgot why we broke up—she couldn't deal with the fact that I was doing something I liked instead of just hanging around all of her loser friends.

Okay, so then who am I going to vote for? Melissa? She's not much better—she won't even talk to me. And I can't vote for Tia because she doesn't even seem interested in going to an East Coast school, which is a major condition of the scholarship. There's Hannah, but all her activities are academic, and even though Maria might admire that, I don't.

So how about Leah? She was sort of quiet during the interview, but she's already applied to a couple of East Coast schools, and she seems really serious about it. But best of all, she isn't my girlfriend, my ex-girlfriend, or even someone I know very well. She deserves a vote just for that.

CHAPTER 7
Not Her Style

"What's the *passé composé* form of *devoir* for *tu?*" Jessica asked, lifting her gaze from the yellow-lined paper on her desk. She looked at Elizabeth, but her sister was lost in some daydream, so she turned to Maria and Tia. But something told her they hadn't even heard her question.

"It's *tu as dû,*" Elizabeth finally responded. Neither Tia nor Maria even turned their heads—they just continued staring into space, doing their best to avoid each other.

"Okay," Elizabeth said, setting her pen down on the desk. "This is stupid. We're supposed to be working *together,* which means we might actually need to speak to each other."

Thank you, Liz, Jessica thought, glancing back and forth between Tia and Maria. But they still didn't say a word.

"All right. What's going on? Why are you two acting like this?" Elizabeth demanded.

"Ask her," Maria said, nodding toward Tia.

"Me?" Tia replied, meeting Maria's gaze for the

first time all period. "You're the one who practically attacked me in drama class."

"Well, you're the one who's competing for a scholarship you don't even care about," Maria shot back.

"What's wrong? Afraid you're going to lose?" Tia asked.

Jessica sat back, shocked to hear her friends sound so immature. This scholarship was bringing out the worst in all of them.

"Um, I just have to say something," she jumped in. "I know this might seem a little hokey, but don't you guys think your friendship is a little more important than who wins this scholarship?"

Tia sighed and lowered her eyes. "But it's not just about who wins," she argued, glancing at Maria. "It's about the fact that brainiac over there thinks she's the only one who deserves to be considered for it in the first place."

"That's not what I said," Maria hissed. "I just think the scholarship should go to someone who actually *wants* it." She turned to Elizabeth. "Come on—you were there, Liz. You heard her answers. How seriously could you take her after she admitted she doesn't even want to go to an East Coast school or that she has no clue what to major in?"

"Oh, that's great," Tia said before Elizabeth could respond. "Put Elizabeth in the middle. As if she'd vote for you after you sat there and practically read your answers from a cue card."

"At least I had answers," Maria snapped.

"Stop it!" Elizabeth blurted out, loudly enough to cause half the class to turn and look at their group.

"*Est-ce qu'il y a une problème, mesdemoiselles*?" Ms. Dalton asked, peering at them over the top of her glasses.

"*Non, Madame Dalton, pardonnez-moi, s'il vous plaît,*" Elizabeth responded with perfect pronunciation.

Ms. Dalton frowned, then returned to the book she was reading while they worked on their group assignments. Jessica glanced around the classroom and winced when she noticed Melissa and her friends watching them with matching little amused smiles.

Jessica leaned in toward Tia and Maria. "Look—can we get through the rest of class without making public spectacles of ourselves?" she asked. "Please?"

"Jessica's right," Elizabeth chimed in. "I mean, at least you guys got *nominated.* I've been hoping for that scholarship for over two years now, and I got completely passed over."

The corner of Tia's mouth twitched, and Maria's angry expression softened.

"Can we just get back to this paragraph?" Jessica suggested. She glanced up at the clock. Only fifteen minutes left—but she had a feeling it would be a long fifteen minutes.

* * *

The second the bell rang at the end of French class, Maria shoved her books into her bag and hopped up, hoping to avoid another confrontation with Tia. She thought about saying something to Elizabeth, but Elizabeth was out of the room faster than she was.

Oh, well, Maria thought, heading to the door right behind her. She could call Elizabeth later and apologize. Yeah, that stuff she'd overheard in the *Oracle* office the other day had bugged her. But if she was in Elizabeth's position, she'd probably be taking all of this even worse.

Just as Maria reached the doorway to the classroom, she felt a light bump from next to her. She turned and saw Melissa standing there.

"What's the matter, Maria?" Melissa asked. "Trying to knock *me* out of the competition since you couldn't convince Tia to drop out?"

Maria tried to keep her face blank, but she cringed inside. Why did Melissa have to overhear their fight?

"Actually, I'm not really worried about competition from someone who thinks Michigan is part of the East Coast," Maria shot back. She pushed her way through the door ahead of Melissa and started down the hall.

"You mean you're not worried at all?" Melissa called after her. "That's strange. Especially considering that I've already beat you in one department."

Maria stopped, the blood rushing in her head.

"You know," Melissa went on, "Ken's really great—you must miss having him around. I'd probably feel sorry for you if I weren't dating him."

Maria's shoulders tensed as she slowly turned around. She noticed that a few other people in the hall were watching her and Melissa. Great—her second public show of the day. This was not her style. But she couldn't let Melissa walk away gloating like that.

"I hope you weren't counting on his vote," Melissa continued. "Because he's moved on, even if you haven't. Although I can understand why it would be harder for you to get over Ken than it would be for him to get over you—you lost a lot more than he did."

Maria swallowed. Was this girl for real? Was this *day* for real?

"Oh, really," Maria managed. Why wasn't anything better coming into her head? Something about Melissa Fox made Maria feel like she was a little kid all over again. The girl was practically half Maria's size, but she had this eerie power to just reduce people to nothing. Maria felt her books beginning to slip in her sweaty palms and readjusted them.

"Well, there's a good comeback," Melissa taunted. "I thought you were supposed to be smart."

"At least my IQ exceeds my shoe size," Maria snapped, finally feeling her brain work again. She heard a few snickers from the crowd around her and winced. Didn't Melissa have to be somewhere? Anywhere?

"Okay, why don't you just let it go," Jessica said, stepping forward and into the gap between Maria and Melissa. Maria hadn't noticed Jessica was there, but at least she was trying to help now. Glancing around, Maria saw Tia standing off to the side, where Jessica had come from.

Please listen to Jessica, Maria thought. But Melissa just rolled her eyes, then walked past Jessica and came up right into Maria's face.

"You're just jealous because you couldn't hold on to your boyfriend—and I can," Melissa stated.

"Are you sure about that?" Maria asked. "Because he came to wish me luck after the interview today."

And then I bit his head off and stormed away, Maria thought. But Melissa didn't need to know about that.

For a second the smug gleam faded from Melissa's clear blue eyes. But she recovered instantly. "I do feel sorry for you," she said. "It must be really hard to let go when someone dumps you so fast like that. You'd grasp at anything to believe he still cares, right?"

Maria gulped. How could Melissa be so mean? Did she stand in front of her mirror at home and practice this stuff?

Everyone around them seemed to be waiting for

Maria to do something, and Melissa was watching her, her eyebrows slightly raised as if inviting another insult that she could turn around and twist back into Maria. But Maria had nothing else to say. All she wanted was to get out of there—but she couldn't let Melissa win. Not again.

"All right, all right," Tia said, striding forward. "Why don't all of you just head to the mall and see if you can buy a life?" she called to the people still standing around watching. Then she grabbed Melissa by the arm.

"Tia—what do you think you're doing?" Melissa protested. She tried to yank her arm free, but Tia wouldn't let go.

"Look—as far as Ken goes, you should probably stop worrying about what Maria's going to do and start thinking about what you're going to tell Will when he comes back to school," Tia said. "You know—Will? Will Simmons? That guy you've been practically *married* to for the past five years?"

Melissa finally jerked her arm away from Tia. "Will already knows about me and Ken. He—"

"So he knows. So what? You think that's going to make things any easier for you?" Tia laughed. She took Melissa's arm again. "Come on, we have to go."

"I am not going *anywhere* with you," Melissa practically squealed. Maria bit back a grin. Watching the girl lose her cool was pretty fun.

"Yes, you are," Tia responded. "Because if you

don't, you're going to be late for cheerleading practice, and as your captain, I can't let you do that." Tia tugged on her elbow again and began to lead her down the hallway past Maria.

When they finally disappeared around the corner, Maria allowed herself to breathe a sigh of relief.

"Wow," Jessica said, coming up next to Maria. "That was cool."

"Very," Maria agreed. She gripped her books tightly, hoping Jessica wouldn't be able to see that her hands were still shaking from that whole confrontation.

"Well, Tia does have a big mouth, but I guess that's not always so bad," Jessica joked. "Not when Melissa's the target." She paused. "Listen, I have to get to practice too," she said. "But are you going to be okay?"

"Yeah," Maria said with a nod. "I'm fine. Go ahead."

Jessica tilted her head, focusing on Maria with an intense stare. "Are you *sure?*" she asked. "Because I know what it's like to do battle with that girl. I've still got the scars."

Maria laughed. "Really. I'm okay," she said. "Go to practice."

"Okay," Jessica said. "But call me later if you need to talk." She turned and headed down the hallway.

Maria took a few seconds to get herself under control, then she started walking toward her locker.

She kept hearing Melissa's voice in her head, taunting her with how fast Ken had jumped from her to Melissa. It hurt way more than she'd want anyone to know. Still, she knew things could have gotten worse—if Tia hadn't gotten rid of Melissa the way she did.

And right after that fight we had in French class too. Maria shook her head. She had been pretty harsh to her friend, but Tia was there when she needed her. She came through—big time. Now Maria just had to figure out a way to show her how much that meant.

Ken strode up the brick pathway that led to Melissa's house, breathing deeply to ease his tense nerves. He looked down at the flowers in his hand, automatically flashing back to the night he'd shown up at Maria's house with a rose. The night they broke up . . . he shook his head, then reached up to press the doorbell. A moment later he heard footsteps approaching, and then the door swung open.

Melissa stood in front of him, her hair pulled back into a neat, clean ponytail. When she saw him, a slight scowl crossed her lips.

"What is it?" she asked, her hand firmly on the knob so she could slam the door shut at any moment.

"I brought you something," Ken offered, lifting up the flowers. Somehow he hadn't been able to bring himself to get Melissa a rose, but the guy at the store had promised him that girls loved these kind of flowers too.

Melissa shifted her weight from one foot to the other, her gaze focused on the flowers. Then she reached out and took them, leaning down to inhale the scent. A small smile tugged at her lips.

"Do you want to come in?" she asked.

He grinned. "Yeah, sure," he said.

He followed her into the house and down the short hall to the living room. They plopped down next to each other on the sofa.

"So what are these for?" Melissa asked as she laid the flowers down on the coffee table.

Ken shrugged. "Just, you know, to say I'm sorry," he said. He inched closer to her. "You were right—I should have been one hundred percent behind you with this scholarship thing. And I wanted to let you know that I am, really."

He meant it too. Melissa understood him. She knew how important playing football was to him and how much he wanted the Michigan scholarship. She even believed he could really go somewhere with football. And that was exactly what he needed—someone who would encourage him. Someone totally different from Maria, who could only cut him down and remind him how big of a loser she thought he was just because he wasn't a brain like her.

"And what about Maria?" Melissa asked, as if

hearing his thoughts. “Where does she fit in?”

“She doesn’t,” he said firmly, meeting Melissa’s gaze. “I’m over Maria. *Completely.* She’s history.”

She paused, staring back at him for a second. “Good,” she finally said. She smiled and squirmed closer to him, tilting her head up to his.

Taking the hint, Ken put his arms around her and pulled her to him. He brushed his lips against hers, letting out a deep sigh as she kissed him back, harder. She seemed to fit against him perfectly, and Ken forgot everything else as he let himself get lost in the kiss.

Elizabeth Wakefield

I have voted for nobody because: I don't think I should have to do this. Mr. Nelson and Mrs. Senate should just choose someone on their own—they're the ones who are going to decide in the end anyway. How important can my vote really be? It probably doesn't count at all.

So I guess I should just write one up and get it over with.

Okay. Well, obviously I can't vote for either Tia or Maria—the way they've been acting about this whole thing just proves that neither one of them deserves it. And Melissa Fox? Give me a break. After what she did to Jessica, I'd say she's more qualified for a prison sentence than a scholarship.

And since I can't vote for myself,

that leaves Leah and Hannah. They were both okay, although Leah was so quiet, I could barely hear her for the first half of the interview. So I guess it's Hannah. There. That's it. I'm done.

Process of elimination—works every time.

CHAPTER 8
SOMETHING TO PROVE

Jade shifted her position in the overstuffed chair in her living room. It was difficult to get comfortable while balancing her notebook and her history textbook on her legs. But if she studied in her room, her mom—who was lying on the sofa, watching some lame made-for-TV movie—might beat her to the phone when her dad called, and Jade couldn't let that happen.

"So what are you studying, honey?" Ms. Wu called without taking her eyes off the television. But before Jade could answer, the telephone rang.

"I'll get it," Jade said, practically leaping from her seat. She grabbed the phone from the coffee table.

"Hello?" she answered, catching her breath.

"Hi, Jade, is your mom around?"

Jade recognized the voice of one of her mother's good friends and held back a groan. "Yeah, sure," she said. She turned to her mom. "It's for you," she said, handing over the receiver.

Jade sat back down in the chair, picking up the books that had fallen to the floor when she jumped up to answer the phone. She pretended to scribble notes down in the margins even though she was listening to every word of her mom's phone call. What if her dad called on the call waiting?

Finally, after what seemed like forever, Ms. Wu said good-bye and hung the phone back up. Almost immediately it rang again.

Ms. Wu started to reach for it, but Jade sprang back up from her seat again. "It's probably for me," she blurted out, grabbing the phone away from her mom.

"Hello?" she said.

"Jade?"

Jade shut her eyes in relief. At least she'd managed to keep her mom from answering.

"You sound out of breath," Mr. Wu said.

"Um, no—just rushing to get the phone," she replied.

"I had no idea you were that excited to talk to me," Mr. Wu said, chuckling. Jade clenched her teeth—she couldn't stand his lame jokes. She glanced over at her mom, who was already engrossed in her movie again.

Good, she thought. Balancing the receiver between her shoulder and chin, she wandered out of the room and down the hall, stretching the cord as far as it would reach.

"Well, anyway," Mr. Wu said, "were you able to get out of work tomorrow night?"

"Oh—yeah," Jade answered. She twisted a strand of black hair around her finger. "I switched shifts with someone else, so I should be able to be home by—" She paused to think about her mother's schedule. Even if Ms. Wu stopped home between jobs tomorrow night, which she usually didn't do, she should be gone by six-thirty. "—seven?" Jade finished.

"Okay, seven it is," Mr. Wu said. "I'll pick you up then, and I'll make our reservation for seven-thirty. You're going to love the restaurant—it's very expensive, but I've been assured it's worth every penny."

Please, Jade thought. Couldn't her father do just one thing without talking about how much it cost?

"So, seven o'clock, then," she said flatly, refusing to give him the satisfaction of responding to his comment.

"Yes," Mr. Wu replied. "I'll see you then."

"Okay," Jade said. "Bye." She leaned back against the cool white wall, holding the receiver down by her waist. Her father just didn't get it. He could take her to the best restaurant in the world, and she would still be miserable. She just didn't want to be around him. Period. Not after the way he'd treated her mom. Not after the way he'd treated *her.*

She shuffled back into the living room and replaced the phone in its cradle.

"What was that all about?" Ms. Wu asked.

"What do you mean?" Jade asked, her muscles tensing.

"You practically tackled me for the phone," Ms. Wu said, sitting up and swinging her legs onto the floor. "Can't I at least find out his name?"

Relax, Jade told herself. Her mom just thought she was wired over some guy. "Um, it was Mike," Jade blurted out, using the first name that popped into her mind. She actually was supposed to call her friend Mike tonight.

"Mike?" Her mom frowned. "Since when are you racing to answer his calls?"

"Well, I thought it might be someone else," Jade explained. She tried to do her best "disappointed" face—eyelids lowered, mouth pouting. "I know, it's stupid," she said, "but for some reason I thought Jeremy might call me tonight—you know, to say he wanted to work things out—and I guess I was just really anxious to get to the phone, that's all."

Ms. Wu tilted her head and pressed her lips together. "Oh, honey," she said. "I'm sorry."

Jade shrugged. "I know he's not going to call," she said. "I just need to get over it."

"You will, I promise," Ms. Wu reassured her. Jade felt guiltier than ever about lying when she saw all the sympathy in her mom's eyes. But she had no choice. There was no way she could admit that she was going to dinner with her dad tomorrow night.

"So," Tia began as she pulled a few of the clean dishes from the dishwasher and stacked them on the counter. "That dinner at Mrs. Senate's house is tomorrow—are you guys planning to come?"

Mr. Ramirez stopped wiping the counter and glanced over at Tia's mom, who was still cleaning up the table.

"Mom?" Tia prodded, realizing that her dad wasn't going to give an answer until he'd heard his wife's opinion.

"Oh, Tia." Mrs. Ramirez moaned, sitting down in one of the chairs. "Are you really going through with this?"

Tia shook her head. "You make it sound like I'm planning to elope or something. This is a *scholarship*—it's supposed to be a good thing."

"It's not that we're not proud of you for being nominated," her father said, stepping closer to Mrs. Ramirez—he was doing that united-front thing parents always did.

"Yeah, I can tell how proud you are from the way you jump for joy every time I bring it up," Tia said. She reached down and pulled out some more dishes, plopping them on top of the others with a gentle clang.

"Tia," her mother scolded. "Don't speak to your father that way."

Tia rolled her eyes. Her parents were being unreasonable—what was she supposed to say?

"Look," her mother continued, "we don't want to tell you what to do—"

"Yeah, right," Tia said. Mrs. Ramirez shot her husband a desperate glance, which Tia recognized as the signal for him to take over.

"No matter what you think, Tia, that's not what we're trying to do," her father said, his voice becoming deeper and more forceful. "We just want you to think this through. If you win, what are you going to do? Traveling across the country for school has never been part of your plan before. We just want to make sure you know what you're doing."

Tia threw up her hands. They sounded just like Maria. "I don't *know* what I want to do, okay? Is that so bad? Why do I have to have everything figured out right now?"

"Because you're competing for a scholarship with very strict requirements. It isn't fair to you or to the other girls competing if you have no intention of meeting them," her mother said.

"But what if I do want to go to an East Coast school?" Tia argued. Even as the words came out, she knew that they weren't really true. She *hadn't* ever considered moving so far away, and she still couldn't imagine actually doing it.

"Then I guess you'll go," Mrs. Ramirez said. She stood up again and continued to clear off the table.

Tia looked over at her dad, who was watching her with a disapproving stare, his eyebrows furrowed together.

"What?" Tia said. "What do you want me to say?"

Mr. Ramirez opened his mouth to speak, but Tia whirled around. "Forget it," she called back over her shoulder, storming out of the kitchen. She was halfway down the hall to her room when she heard Miguel and Tomás arguing in front of the door to the bedroom they shared.

"Tia!" Tomás yelled when she reached the door. "Miguel won't give me my truck back."

Tia groaned. "Miguel, give him the truck," she ordered.

"I just want to see how it works," Miguel said, holding the truck up high so Tomás couldn't reach it.

"Tia!" Tomás protested, breaking into tears as he jumped for the truck.

"Miguel!" Tia shouted. "You *know* how it works—it used to be *yours*. But it's Tomás's now; you gave it to him months ago."

"I know," Miguel said, hanging his head sheepishly. "But I want to play with it."

Tia rolled her eyes. "You only want it because he has it. If Tomás didn't want it, you wouldn't want it either," she said. She grabbed the truck from Miguel and handed it back to Tomás, then walked past them into her bedroom. She slammed the door shut behind her and flopped down onto her bed.

Sometimes her brothers really drove her crazy. They were always fighting over things they didn't even *want*—just to see who could win or to show that they weren't about to back down.

Tia squeezed her eyes shut, trying to block out the realization that suddenly hit her. But she couldn't push it away.

I've been acting like my brothers. Everyone was right—Maria, her parents. She didn't want the Senate scholarship, or at least all the requirements that came with it.

How did this happen? Last week she'd known that she wanted to go to college close to home. When had everything gotten so mixed up?

Tia thought back to her meeting with Mr. Nelson, when he'd first told her about the scholarship. Even then she'd had her doubts, but she had ignored them. It was a *full scholarship*—how could she have seriously considered *not* going for it? And then, when Maria had acted so surprised that Tia was competing for it—and her parents too—Tia had felt like . . . well, like she had something to prove.

Tia opened her eyes and reached over the side of her bed. There was a stack of papers on the floor, and she was pretty sure her original information form for the Senate scholarship was there. She thumbed through the papers, scattering the pile all over her carpet, but she finally found it.

The winner must attend an approved college from the list included, and while there she shall maintain a GPA of 3.5 or above, participate in a minimum of six activities, and be a leader in the college community.

She dropped the form back onto the floor. What

had she been thinking? She didn't want to commit to any of that. She wanted to go someplace like Berkeley and make new friends. She wanted to take road trips into San Francisco and drive home every other weekend to play with her brothers. She wanted to fail a class or drop a class or take a class just for the fun of it and not have to worry about losing her scholarship. But somewhere along the line she'd forgotten all that and ended up hurting her friends and her family—the very people that were most important to her.

It's not too late to fix this, she decided. She sat up, running her hand through her long hair. First thing tomorrow morning she was going to pull herself out of the competition.

"Go away—I'm sleeping," Elizabeth called out in response to the knock on her bedroom door. She was completely awake—doing her English reading—but she was not up for company, especially if it meant listening to how happy her sister was with Jeremy Aames.

The door opened anyway, and Jessica walked in, holding the cordless phone. She frowned when she saw Elizabeth sitting at her desk. "Sleeping. Right," she said. "Whatever. Maria's on the phone for you."

Elizabeth closed her eyes. *Great,* she thought. *Probably trying to convince me to vote for her. I wonder if she's calling all the judges tonight.* She opened her eyes, ready to ask her sister to give Maria an excuse, but Jessica was gone. The phone, however, was lying on her dresser.

"Thanks, Jess," Elizabeth muttered. She got up and walked over to the dresser, then snatched up the phone. "Hello," she said as she brought the receiver to her ear.

"Hi, Liz," Maria started. "Thanks for talking to me. I wouldn't blame you if you didn't want to—I was way out of line today. I'm sorry."

"Oh," Elizabeth said, taken off guard. "It's okay." She strolled over to her bed and perched on the edge, fingering a loose thread dangling down from her comforter.

"So, I just wanted to let you know that and also to tell you . . . well, I'm going to drop out of the scholarship competition."

Elizabeth sat up straight. "You're what?"

"First thing tomorrow," Maria said. "I'm going to Mr. Nelson to tell him I want out."

Was she going totally insane? Who would turn down an opportunity like that?

"But—why?" Elizabeth asked. She scooted farther back on the bed, pulling her legs under her.

"I don't know," Maria replied. "I mean, I guess I do. You missed it earlier, but Tia stood up for me after French class when Melissa tried to tear me apart in the hall. It was really cool, and it just made me think about how I've been treating her and you. I've been a really bad friend, and Jessica's right—our friendships mean a lot more than this scholarship."

Elizabeth didn't know what to say. She wasn't sure she'd be able to give up a chance for the Senate scholarship, and she knew that Maria was at least as driven—if not more—than she was.

"That's really nice of you," she began. "But Maria, this is the Senate scholarship—you and I have been talking about it since junior year."

"I know," Maria said. "Trust me, this isn't easy—the scholarship means a lot to me. But I guess I finally realized that my friends mean more. I don't want you to have to worry about who to vote for, and I don't want to compete against Tia."

Elizabeth smiled. After everything that had happened with Conner in the beginning of the year, she'd been worried that she and Maria would never be as close as they used to be again. It was nice to see that their friendship was stronger than ever. Still, it was way too big a sacrifice—she was sure Tia would never expect Maria to do this.

"Listen, Maria, I just think—"

"Liz, I'm going to let you go before you talk me out of it," Maria interrupted. "I just wanted you to know tonight. I'm going to tell Tia tomorrow morning. Okay?"

"Um, yeah, okay," Elizabeth said. They hung up, and Elizabeth stared at the phone for a second, still in shock. Maria, one of the most competitive people she'd ever met, was actually going to drop out of the scholarship competition? For her friends?

Elizabeth fell back on her bed, blinking at the ceiling. She wondered again if she'd be strong enough to do the same thing in Maria's position. *Probably not,* she told herself, judging by how selfish she'd been all week. In some ways she'd been worse than Maria—so caught up in her own little pity party that she'd never even considered voting for one of her friends because she was too jealous that they'd been nominated and she hadn't.

But maybe it wasn't too late. If she could just admit to herself that she wasn't nominated because she wasn't the best candidate, maybe then she could sit down and vote for the right person. *Instead of just choosing the only person I've never met.*

Elizabeth Wakefield

I have voted for Maria Slater because:

Of all the candidates nominated for this honor, I believe Maria is the most qualified. During her four years at SVH she has demonstrated her commitment to excellence by achieving high grades while participating in several activities, and she has always done so by giving 100 percent to everything she does—and that includes her friendships. Maria has such a strong sense of character that she actually considered pulling out of the competition for this scholarship—which means a great deal to her—simply because she didn't want to stand in the way of one of her friends. And by the way, if she does try to withdraw herself from this competition, she shouldn't be allowed to. She deserves this honor, and she has earned it. Maria is an incredible student and a strong leader, and I am confident she will be successful in anything she pursues.

Ken Matthews

All right. One more time through—this time for real.

~~Hannah Galloway:~~ too academic, not well-rounded enough

~~Tia Ramirez:~~ well-rounded and outgoing but didn't seem really committed to the whole idea of going to a competitive school

~~Leah Castellana:~~ good but too quiet—not really into leadership stuff

Melissa Fox: well-rounded, could handle a competitive school if she won, outgoing, involved

Maria Slater: well-rounded, outgoing, definitely into the East Coast competitive school thing, will probably be famous someday, and definitely deserves it

Great, I'm down to two, and guess who they are? So, should I pick my girlfriend or my ex-girlfriend? Or maybe I should just flip a coin. I could fake a flu and skip school tomorrow—then maybe Mr. Nelson would just figure this out without my vote.

CHAPTER 9
Team Effort

"Tia!"

Tia stopped and looked around the nearly empty hallway. She didn't recognize anyone, but she was sure she'd heard her name.

"Tia!"

This time Tia spotted Maria jogging out of Mr. Collins's homeroom. *Good.* This was her chance to tell her that she was stepping aside, pulling out of a competition she really hadn't belonged in from the start.

"Hey, Maria," Tia said. She hesitated, trying to guess Maria's mood. She wasn't up for another round of biting each other's heads off. "So, what's up?" she asked awkwardly.

Maria shrugged. "Um, nothing, really," she said. She didn't seem angry, but she wasn't acting natural either. "So, what are you doing wandering the halls during homeroom anyway?" she asked.

"Oh—I just got done talking to Mr. Nelson," Tia explained, holding out her pink late pass as evidence.

"Mr. Nelson?" Maria asked, her eyes narrowing.

Here it comes. She'd better just blurt out her news fast, before Maria had a chance to lay into her again.

"Yeah," Tia replied. "In fact, I'm glad I ran into you. I—"

"Me too," Maria interrupted, "because there's something I need to tell you. About the scholarship."

Tia shook her head. "Maria, before you say anything, just let me—"

"I'm dropping out," Maria cut in.

"You're what?" Tia asked. She took a step backward, her mind reeling. Why would Maria do that?

"I'm pulling out of the competition," Maria explained. "I'm on my way to see Mr. Nelson right now, to give him this." She pulled a piece of crisp paper out of the notebook she was holding and passed it to Tia.

Tia scanned the neatly typed words, unable to believe what she was reading.

> Dear Mrs. Senate—
>
> I wanted to thank you, Mr. Nelson, and the faculty of Sweet Valley High for giving me the opportunity to compete for the Lydia G. Senate scholarship. I am greatly honored.
>
> This scholarship is an amazing and generous gift to the students of Sweet Valley, and I'm sure the winner—whoever she may be—will be forever grateful for the chance

to pursue an excellent education at a first-rate school.

I regret, however, that I have found it necessary to withdraw myself from this competition due to personal reasons. I realize that this is rather late notice, but I feel that my withdrawal from the competition is not only in my best interests, but also the best interests of the other candidates.

Once again, thank you for this opportunity.

Sincerely,

Maria Slater

"Oh my God, Maria," Tia said, staring up at her friend. "But . . . why? What do you mean"—she paused to glance down at the letter—" 'the best interests of the other candidates'?"

Maria shrugged. "I guess I just realized that winning this scholarship isn't the most important thing in the world. In fact, it wouldn't mean anything to me if I lost my friends in the process."

"You mean . . . you're doing this for *me?*"

Maria gave her a small smile. "Yeah—in a way. But I'm doing it for me too. I don't like the way I was acting, and I needed to find a way to stop."

Suddenly Tia started to laugh. Maria frowned, obviously confused.

"What's so funny?" she asked.

Tia tried to contain her giggles so she could talk.

"Well," she said when she'd regained her composure. "I guess that whole 'great minds' line is kind of on target here."

Maria's frown deepened. "I don't . . ."

She trailed off as Tia held out Maria's letter, then began tearing it in half.

"Tia!" Maria shouted. Her jaw dropped. "What are you doing?"

"I'm ripping up your letter," Tia stated. She put the two halves together and ripped them into quarters.

"That took me an hour to write!" Maria protested.

"Well, then you wasted an hour," Tia responded. "Because you're not dropping out of the competition."

"Why not?" Maria asked, a note of frustration creeping into her tone.

Tia grinned. "Because I already did."

Maria's dark eyes filled with shock. "You did?"

Tia nodded. "I had my mom drop me off early so I could talk to Mr. Nelson," she said.

Maria shifted her books higher in her arms. "Well, what did he say?" she asked.

"I don't think he was thrilled that I waited until now to tell him I wasn't interested," Tia said. "But he understood. And he said I could still come to the dinner tonight—so I'll be there to cheer you on!"

Maria giggled, but her expression still seemed unsure. "I don't get it, though—why did *you* decide to drop out?" she asked.

"Are you kidding?" Tia asked. She blew a wisp of hair off her forehead. "I don't want to go to an East Coast school—I never did. This scholarship isn't right for me—but it's got your name written all over it. And you *deserve* it."

Maria's face finally relaxed into a wide smile. "Thank you so much, Tia. I'm so sorry for all the things I said to you this week. I—"

Tia held up her palm to stop Maria. "I'll forget what you said if you forget what I said," she offered.

"Deal," Maria responded.

"Good. Now, let's go tell Liz," Tia said, grabbing Maria by the hand and pulling her down the hall.

Maria chuckled. "You know, you're getting really good at this dragging-people-away thing," she teased.

Tia looked back over her shoulder and grinned. "I have little brothers," she said. "Trust me—I get a lot of practice."

Jade strolled across the courtyard with her plastic cafeteria tray, scanning the area for a private spot. She couldn't really deal with another earful of happy-in-love Jeremy stories from Jessica, especially when all she could think about was dinner with her dad tonight.

She had started to head toward an open area in the sun when she caught sight of Evan Plummer sitting under a tree—alone.

This could be interesting, she thought, changing

direction. After all, a cute guy could always give some good distraction.

"Hey, there," she said as she got closer. "Room for one more?"

Evan gazed up at her, squinting at first, but then his eyes widened with recognition. "Oh—you're Jessica's friend. Jade, right?" he asked.

Jessica's friend? It wasn't exactly the way Jade would have introduced herself, but at least he remembered her.

"Yeah." She nodded, smiling. "So . . . can I join you?"

"Sure, of course," he said. He picked up his lunch tray and moved it to his other side, then shoved his backpack over to make a space for Jade.

Jade set her food down first, then sat down with her back against the tree—close enough to Evan so that he could probably catch a whiff of her light perfume, but not so close that she'd make him uncomfortable. She'd nailed down the art of wrapping a guy around her finger a long time ago.

"Salad, huh?" she asked, eyeing Evan's tray. All kinds of healthy ingredients were heaped onto his plate—she could see lettuce, spinach leaves, peppers, mushrooms, tomatoes, and sprouts. "Impressive," she commented. "I always go for the fries," she added, pointing at her own tray.

Evan glanced down at his plate and shrugged. "I just can't make myself buy the fries," he replied, shaking his head. "I mean, what you've got there is essentially one medium potato, right?"

"I guess," Jade said.

"So that would cost about thirty cents at the store, and if you took it home and baked it, it would actually be pretty good for you as long as you didn't slather it with too much butter or anything, right?"

Jade blinked. "Um . . . yeah." Where exactly was Evan going here? He hadn't seemed this serious the other day.

"But when that same potato gets made into fries," Evan continued, "you pay five times as much for a vegetable that's been soaked in oil and salted until it's nothing but fat and sodium. It's such a waste. In a lot of ways that poor little potato"—he pointed directly at Jade's french fries—"symbolizes the reckless consumerism that plagues America. We spend huge amounts of money on goods that don't even begin to satisfy our most basic needs."

"Oo-kay," she said, wondering if she'd made the wrong decision to sit with him. Distraction was one thing—a lecture on American society was another. "So, then, I guess it would be stupid of me to offer you one," she joked, trying to lighten the mood.

"Oh, not at all," Evan responded in the same solemn tone. Then he reached over and grabbed two of her fries, popping them into his mouth.

"I *like* them," he said once he'd swallowed. "I just

can't buy them." He grinned at her, then took a sip from his water.

Jade shook her head. Then, almost against her will, the corners of her mouth curved into a smile. "Jessica didn't tell me you were—"

"So political?" Evan interrupted.

"*Nooo*—such a freak," Jade said with a laugh.

Evan grinned and started to laugh too, once again treating Jade to the sight of his perfectly straight, white teeth.

"I'm surprised," Evan said when he stopped laughing. "Because Jessica told me a few things about you."

Jade almost choked on the fry she'd just stuck in her mouth. Had Evan asked Jessica about her? She quickly gulped down the mushy pieces. "Like what?" she asked.

"Not much. Just that you stole the love of her life and then helped her get him back."

"Oh," Jade blurted out, feeling her cheeks get unusually warm. Jade Wu did *not* blush.

Evan helped himself to another one of her fries, apparently pleased with himself for setting her off balance like that.

"That was pretty recent, right?" Evan persisted.

"Um . . . yeah, but . . ." What was she supposed to say? Why did he even care? She glanced down at the ground, feeling an unexpected wave of hurt. Every time she thought she was over the whole thing, it would sneak up on her.

"Oh, hey, I'm sorry," he said. "That's got to be rough. I probably shouldn't have brought it up."

"Oh, no, that's okay," Jade said. If Evan thought she was still hung up on Jeremy, he'd probably pass the info along to Jessica—which would not be good. She and Jessica were finally starting to be friends again, and it would only make things awkward. Besides, she *was* getting over Jeremy. It was more the way things ended that made her upset—feeling like he'd stayed with her only out of pity when he really wanted someone else.

Time for a topic change, she decided. Guys didn't like girls who got emotional so easily. *Maybe I'll ask him if there are any other vegetables he cares about as passionately as the potato,* she thought, her smile returning.

But before she could say anything, he started to stand up. "Sorry to eat and run," he said, "but I have to meet with my swim coach." He hefted his backpack onto one shoulder and picked up his lunch tray. "But if you ever need someone to help you finish your fries again . . ."

"I know where to go," she finished for him.

Evan flashed her another smile, then turned and headed across the grass. Jade slumped back against the tree, trying to remember everything Jessica had told her about Evan yesterday. She and Evan had dated for a little while, then decided to be friends, and then the same thing had happened between

Evan and Elizabeth. So what was the deal? Did Evan only go for blondes?

That would be pretty narrow-minded for such a politically correct guy, Jade thought, smiling to herself as she munched on another french fry.

But so what if he did? That was okay. In fact, it was good. Because there was nothing Jade liked more than a challenge. If anyone could convince Evan that girls with dark hair were way cooler than blondes, it was Jade. And that was just what she was going to do. Once her father was back in Oregon, where he belonged.

". . . forty-two . . . forty-three . . . forty-four . . ." Will exhaled with each crunch, feeling his stomach muscles contracting a little more each time.

"Will—you have a few visitors," Mrs. Simmons called from the foot of the stairway. Quickly Will scrambled onto his one good leg and hopped over to his bed. The pain in his right knee was intense, but somehow he managed to sit back and swing both legs up onto the deep green comforter. He wiped at his brow with a white T-shirt that had been sitting on his bed, then tossed it into the laundry basket on the far side of his room. By the time he heard foot-steps reach the top of the stairs, he had grabbed a magazine so it would look like he'd just been hang-ing out and resting.

Will glanced at the alarm clock on his nightstand.

It was four-thirty on a Friday afternoon. Who would be coming to visit him now?

Cheering practice would be over by now, he couldn't help thinking. He'd played it out several times in his head already—the way Melissa would come over and beg his forgiveness for the way she betrayed him.

But when his door swung open, Melissa wasn't there. Instead Josh Radinsky and Matt Wells came bounding into his room.

"Will—hey, what's up?" Josh said.

"Hey, man, how's it going?" Matt added before Will had a chance to respond. They walked over to Will's bed and slapped him high fives that turned into casual handshakes. Then Josh grabbed the chair from Will's desk and flipped it around so he could sit straddling it next to the bed. Matt plopped down on the edge of the bed, turning to face Will.

"Not bad, not bad," Will told them, feeling an easy smile creep onto his face. Matt and Josh had obviously come straight from practice. They had changed their clothes and probably showered, too, but their cheeks were still flushed from their workouts. Friday practices when there was no Saturday game were the hardest—Coach always figured they had the weekend to recover.

"So how's the knee?" Josh asked, gesturing toward Will's right leg, which he'd elevated on a pile of pillows.

"It's okay," Will said with a shrug. "It's actually feeling pretty good today." *If you forget about that constant throbbing pain,* he thought.

"Cool," Matt said, nodding. "Any idea when you're coming back to school?"

Will looked down at his hands and flicked an imaginary piece of dirt out from under his thumbnail. Dr. Goldstein had cleared him to go back a while ago, but he'd been making excuses. Just that morning he'd finally decided he was ready, but he hadn't anticipated having to tell anyone else about it so soon—and he wasn't sure he wanted to.

"Um . . . yeah, well—my doctor actually told me today that I could go back as early as Monday if I'm feeling okay, but it's not a sure thing yet," he lied. He knew going back to school wasn't going to be easy, and he didn't want to commit himself to anything he wasn't sure he could follow through on.

"Monday? That's awesome," Josh said, giving Will another high five.

"I knew that knee injury wouldn't keep you down long," Matt added with a grin.

"Yeah, well, you know." Will shrugged. "I've been getting around pretty well on crutches—so as long as I can keep that up . . ."

"Oh, man," Josh said. "Wait until I tell the rest of the guys—they're going to be so psyched you're coming back."

Will's eyebrows shot up. "They are?"

"Yeah, totally," Matt agreed. "Matthews isn't bad, but it's not the same without you there. Besides—the guy's ego is getting too big already. We need you there to keep it in check."

Josh glared at Matt, and Will saw his jaw clench.

"What?" Matt asked. He frowned in confusion, then glanced back at Will. "Oh, I'm sorry, man," he said, finally getting it. "I didn't mean to bring up—"

"It's all right," Will said, waving a hand in the air. "I'm going to have to see him sooner or later."

Him, Will thought, *and Melissa.* But he knew neither one of his buddies was stupid enough to bring up *her* name. The silence hung between them for a few seconds, and Matt shifted uncomfortably on the bed.

"Seriously, though," Matt went on. "You *should* come to practice on Monday. Everyone would be really pumped to see you."

"You think so?" Will asked. Nobody had really been by much since he'd gotten out of the hospital. He had begun to think they had all forgotten him. Or that maybe they were doing better with Ken as quarterback. When he'd dragged himself to the homecoming game, the number of welcome-back-Ken signs had made him feel sick.

"Yeah," Josh answered. "It would do a lot for the team. I mean, we've been playing okay and everything, but it doesn't feel like as much of a team effort without you calling the plays."

"Really?" Will asked, narrowing his eyes.

"Absolutely," Matt said. "You've got to come—it'll really mean a lot to the guys."

Will glanced back and forth between his friends, unsure what to say. He knew it would probably be good for him to see all his friends again too. But there was still the fact that Ken would be out there in his position, calling his plays and making his passes.

"Yeah, well . . ." Will scratched the back of his neck. "I'll, um, definitely stop by—you know, if I'm still feeling up to it by the end of the day," he couldn't help adding. Watching Ken would be hard, but there would be one other bonus to going to football practice on Monday, aside from seeing his teammates. Will knew that the cheerleaders always practiced right next to the football field, which meant Melissa would be there, watching.

She'd see him talking with the guys, messing around, and walking—with his crutches, but still. And when she did, Will was certain she'd realize just how much she'd lost when she turned her back on him.

Elizabeth Wakefield

To: tee@swiftnet.com
From: lizw@cal.rr.com
Subject: Free meal!

Tia—

The dinner at Mrs. Senate's house starts at six-thirty, so I thought I'd pick you up at five forty-five—sound okay?

Oh, and BTW, I know I said it before, but I think it's really cool the way you pulled yourself out of the competition and convinced Maria to stay in. You really are a good friend. :)

See you soon,

Liz

PS Maria's riding to the dinner with her parents, but I was thinking maybe we could take her out afterward for either a celebration or a consolation—what do you think?

TIA RAMIREZ

To: lizw@cal.rr.com
From: tee@swiftnet.com
Subject: re: free meal!

Hey Liz–

Five forty-five will be perfect.

Thanks! You're a great friend, too! :)

And yes, we should definitely take Maria out, but think positive–it's going to be a celebration all the way!

Adios,

Tee

CHAPTER 10
And the Winner Is . . .

"Thank you," Jade said, smiling at the busboy who'd just refilled her water glass for the millionth time. It seemed like every time she took a sip, he was there in a second to replenish her supply.

The busboy gave a small nod and bowed slightly, then he was gone.

"They don't expect you to engage in conversation," Mr. Wu said with an amused smile.

"*They?*" Jade asked, irritated by her dad's tone.

"The wait staff," Mr. Wu explained. "At restaurants of this caliber the service is supposed to be imperceptible." He cast a casual glance toward the left side of the room, and Jade followed his gaze. There were ten men and women in identical black pants, white shirts, and black bow ties lined up against the wall. Their blank expressions reminded her of the guards at Buckingham Palace she'd seen on TV.

"Everything you need simply appears at your table, without even one word exchanged," Mr. Wu continued. "It's the way dining out should always be—as opposed to those cheap diners where every customer knows about Betty Lou's new boyfriend and the orders are shouted into the kitchen from the counter."

"I like diners," Jade said flatly.

"Yes, well, I'm sure your tastes will mature someday," her father assured her.

One more hour and he'll be gone, Jade reminded herself as she struggled not to scream. Starting an argument would just make the night last longer, and there was no way she was going to risk that.

Jade took a sip from her crystal water glass and enjoyed the piano music coming from the far corner. It actually was a very nice restaurant, although she'd never admit that to her father. The chairs were padded with crushed green velvet that matched the rest of the room perfectly, and each table had a beautiful view of the bay and the boats that were moored along the wooden docks. If she were here on a date with a cute guy—someone like Evan Plummer, maybe—she'd probably be having a great time.

Mr. Wu cleared his throat. "So," he began. "Is your mom still driving that beat-up green station wagon she bought just after the divorce?"

Oh, great, Jade thought. *Here we go again.* So far Mr. Wu had managed to criticize the fact that Jade lived in an apartment instead of a house, attended a public school instead of a private school, and worked in a pizza place instead of a corporate company where she could begin to make important connections. Apparently her mom's car was next in the line of fire.

"Yes. She does," Jade said, pressing her lips together and bracing for the next comment.

"Really? Because I didn't see it parked outside the building tonight." Mr. Wu cocked his head. "Does she have a reserved space in the back?"

Jade snorted. *Yeah, right. And we have valet parking too.* "No—our building doesn't have reserved spaces—it's street parking only." Jade spoke as if she were explaining the concept to a five-year-old. "Mom's car wasn't there because she wasn't home."

Mr. Wu wrinkled his brow. "Is she *ever* home?" he asked.

"Of course she is," Jade snapped. She was quickly reaching the limit of tolerating her dad's constant criticism. It was one thing for him to complain about the way Jade lived her life, but when he started picking on her mother, that was it. She couldn't take it anymore. "Mom's home a lot, and we spend tons of time together. The only reason she wasn't around tonight is because she's at work." She leaned forward and narrowed her eyes at her father. "Did you even know that she's working two jobs now?"

Mr. Wu sat back in his chair and gazed at Jade, his eyebrows knit together. "No. I hadn't realized that. I—"

"Well, she is," Jade interrupted. "It's not easy getting by on one income—not that I'd expect you to understand that. I mean, you're living happily in Oregon with your new wife and your Mercedes—what would you know about scraping money together for the rent payment? Especially considering that you only pay minimum child support—*none* if I'm not holding down a job."

Mr. Wu opened his mouth to speak, but Jade kept going. "Yeah, Mom's been running herself ragged over the last few weeks. In fact, she's been working so many hours that she even ended up in the hospital for a few days. Did you realize *that?*"

Mr. Wu raised his eyebrows and blinked a few times. "Uh, no, I . . . I didn't," he said slowly. He cleared his throat and shifted uncomfortably. "Is she all right?"

Jade took a long sip of cool water. "Yeah, she's fine now," she said with a shrug. Finally she'd managed to fluster her dad. It was about time he realized how hard her mother worked.

For the next few minutes Mr. Wu kept his focus on the menu, but Jade could see something different in his eyes—something more *human.* What she'd said seemed to have actually gotten to him. Was it possible that Mr. Insensitivity actually cared about his ex-wife?

No, that can't be it, Jade told herself, dropping her own eyes down to her menu. *He's just rewriting that conversation in his memory so he can go home to Oregon feeling good about the money he dropped on this dinner.*

But Jade didn't care. Mr. Wu could go ahead and rewrite the last seven years—in his head. As long as he kept quiet, she was fine.

Maria felt her hands begin to shake as Mrs. Senate glided up to the podium at the front of her spacious dining room. The room was more like a banquet hall. Crystal chandeliers hung from the ceiling, and the other nominees, their parents, the student judges, and various faculty members were seated around ten round tables spaced across the hardwood floor.

"This is the moment you've all been waiting for," Mrs. Senate said as she unfolded a sheet of paper. The entire crowd seemed to shift collectively as Mrs. Senate spoke. Maria glanced around her table at Tia, Hannah, Leah, and Melissa. She caught Tia's eye, and Tia flashed her an encouraging smile.

"I want to thank you all for coming tonight," Mrs. Senate began, nodding to the audience. Her thick, white hair was smoothed back into a neat bun, and the only jewelry she wore was a simple strand of pearls with matching earrings. As Maria watched her, she wondered if someday *she* would be a graceful woman at the podium about to award a generous scholarship.

"And I want to thank our nominees for their outstanding applications. They all deserve to be recognized for their efforts." Mrs. Senate brought her hands together, and the audience joined her in a round of applause. "And now," she continued when the clapping had subsided, "without further ado, it is time to announce this year's recipient of the Lydia G. Senate scholarship."

Tia reached over and grabbed Maria's hand, squeezing it tightly, and Maria squeezed it back. From the next table over, Maria could feel Elizabeth's gaze, and when she turned, Elizabeth gave her a subtle thumbs-up. Maria tried to smile, but it came out more like she was wincing. Her heart was pounding so fast, she was afraid she was going to hyperventilate.

"This year's recipient," Mrs. Senate continued, reading from her paper, "is a remarkable young woman. Not only has she maintained an extremely high grade-point average throughout her high-school career, but she has also been involved in numerous extracurricular activities." Maria breathed deeply and squeezed Tia's hand tighter. It could still be any one of them. Part of her wanted to stand up and beg Mrs. Senate to just announce the winner—put them all out of their misery.

"She has participated in student government, the National Honor Society, girls' track, and the school newspaper, to name a few."

I've done all of those, Maria thought, a shudder running through her body.

"Her teachers describe her as a dynamic student. A leader. A young woman who is motivated to succeed and who has already achieved great success in her life—most recently as the stunning lead in the Sweet Valley High school play."

Maria gripped Tia's hand even tighter as the butterflies in her stomach intensified. *It's me,* Maria thought. *She's talking about me.* But at the same time she couldn't believe it was possible. She'd wanted this scholarship for so long—how could it really be happening?

On a sudden, strange instinct Maria shifted her gaze over to the student-judges' table. Her breath caught when she saw Ken staring right at her. Their eyes met for a second, and Ken started to smile. She felt herself smiling in return and quickly looked away.

"As I said before," she heard Mrs. Senate say, "all of our nominees this year were outstanding, but as one of the student judges wrote, no one is more deserving of this award than . . . Maria Slater," Mrs. Senate finished with a smile. "Maria, could you come up here?"

Maria tried to stand, but her legs felt too weak. Tia had already jumped up and begun to clap wildly, but Maria simply couldn't move. It all seemed too unreal.

"You did it, Maria!" Tia squealed. Her voice was nearly lost in the applause from the audience. Everyone was standing now, and Elizabeth got up and ran over to her, helping her stand. The room was buzzing, and as Maria glanced around, she was amazed to see everyone looking at *her.* It was better than any curtain call she'd ever experienced.

"Oh my God," she whispered. "I really won."

Elizabeth and Tia both threw their arms around her.

"Of course you did!" Tia told her.

Maria stared at her friends. "I can't believe it," she said.

"You'd better believe it," Elizabeth said, grinning as she leaned in closer, "because you've got to go up there and make an acceptance speech now."

"Yeah, but keep it short," Tia added. "Because we're taking you out to celebrate as soon as this is over."

Maria laughed. "You guys are the best," she told them, grasping both of their hands. Then after shooting a quick smile at her parents, who were still applauding madly, Maria turned and began to walk toward the podium.

From somewhere behind her she heard Melissa's voice—probably taking one last jab at her—but all Maria could do was smile. Nothing could possibly get her down tonight—not even anything Melissa had to say.

Maria felt like she was floating all the way to the front of the room. She stepped up to the podium, accepting a hug from Mrs. Senate.

"Congratulations," Mrs. Senate whispered in her ear as she pulled away.

"Thanks," Maria said. She turned to look at the audience, focusing on Tia and Elizabeth and their wide, supportive smiles. She couldn't even believe how many things had changed this year. But at least she'd come through it all with two really amazing friends.

And now—partly because of them—she was on her way to an exciting future.

"So," Mr. Wu said, glancing up and down the street outside Jade's apartment complex from the comfort of his leather driver's seat. "I guess your mother's still out."

"She's working, remember?" Jade said through gritted teeth.

Doesn't he ever let up? she wondered, easing herself out of the Mercedes. She slammed the passenger door shut and leaned down to speak through the open window. "Besides, she'll be home soon."

"Are you sure you'll be all right?"

What am I—six?

"Yes, I'll be fine. I'm seventeen, you know," she added, figuring her father probably still thought of her as the little kid he left behind all those years ago.

"Mm-hmm." Mr. Wu nodded, barely reacting. Either he was getting really good at dealing with Jade's sarcasm, or his mind was already back in Oregon. Jade suspected it was the second choice.

"Well—thanks for dinner. Have a good flight," she offered.

Again Mr. Wu just nodded, his dark eyes directed at her but not really focused. He'd been spacing out like this all night. Not that it was all that shocking that he didn't find his daughter too interesting. He never had before.

"All right, then," Mr. Wu said. He lifted one hand from the steering wheel in a weak wave. "I'll talk with you soon."

"Yep," Jade agreed, backing away. And then finally her father's silver Mercedes—the rented one that wasn't nearly as nice as the one he drove at home—pulled away and disappeared in the distance.

"I survived," she muttered to herself as she turned to walk up to her apartment. And surviving that meant one thing—she definitely deserved a major reward.

Jade Wu

Instant Message

JaWu:	Hey, sorry I forgot to call you last night. I got distracted by something annoying. What are you doing home on a Friday night?
MikeyB:	Holding down the fort—my parents went away for the weekend. But what do you mean, night? It's not even nine yet.
JaWu:	Does that mean you're up for something?
MikeyB:	Depends. What do you want to do?
JaWu:	How about the Riot?
MikeyB:	Possibility. Maybe there will be some SVH girls there you can introduce me to.
JaWu:	Hello? I need a serious dance partner, and I'm not in the mood to hook you up with anyone anyway.
MikeyB:	Okay, okay—don't bite my head off. Guess someone had a bad day.
JaWu:	Yeah, you could say that. But I don't want to talk about it—I just want to dance!
MikeyB:	Sounds good. Meet you by the bar

on the first floor in a half hour?

JaWu: Perfect. And no drooling over other girls—you're with me tonight.

MikeyB: Yeah, yeah. Whatever. But you owe me one. . . .

JaWu: Actually, I think you still owe me, but we can talk about that at the Riot. See you there!

CHAPTER 11

No Excuse

"That was hysterical," Jade sputtered, laughing so hard, she could barely speak. "And then he spilled his drink all over that woman in the spandex!"

Mike doubled over in the middle of her apartment development's courtyard. "I thought you were going to totally lose it," he said.

"Me?" Jade asked. "You're the one who almost fell out of your seat when she said, 'That's okay—it's waterproof!' "

Mike clutched at his stomach with one hand and cupped the other one over his mouth, trying to keep himself from making too much noise.

"Stop it—don't make me laugh." He moaned. "My stomach's still reeling from those nachos."

He looked so ridiculous—standing there shaking with laughter and wincing at the same time—that Jade nearly started giggling all over again too. She'd forgotten how much fun she and Mike used to have when they'd been next-door neighbors back in Palisades. He was one of the only guy friends she had that she'd never dated, probably because they became friends when they were little kids.

"Well, here we are," Jade said, fidgeting with her key in the lock. "Thanks for walking me to the door." She really didn't like coming home alone at night, although she never would have admitted it to her father—or her mother. But Mike was cool about stuff like that, and he'd offered to follow her home and make sure she got in okay.

"No problem," Mike said, then suddenly he leaned forward, grabbing at his stomach. "Oh, man." He groaned.

Jade frowned. "Mike? Are you okay?"

He glanced up at her, and even in the half-light of the moon she could see his face was pretty pale. "I'm not feeling so great," he admitted.

"Why don't you come in and just sit for a little while?" she offered. She unlocked the door, and they walked inside together. As soon as they made it to the living room, Mike collapsed onto the sofa, still holding his stomach.

"It must be those nachos," he said, his face screwed up in pain. "They really knocked me out."

Jade shifted her weight. "I *told* you they tasted funny," she pointed out. "I wanted to send them back, but *nooo,* you didn't want to annoy the cute waitress—so instead you finished the whole platter by yourself."

Mike looked up at her and grimaced. "You

know—when you rant like that, you sound just like my mom."

Jade grabbed a pillow from the side of the couch and batted him on the shoulder. "Come on!" Mike protested. "I'm sick here."

Jade rolled her eyes, but she put the pillow away. "So what are you going to do? You can't drive home like that," she said.

"Yeah," Mike said. "I don't think I can. Would it be okay if I crashed here for the night? I could drive home first thing in the morning."

Jade shrugged. She didn't care, and her mother wouldn't either if she were home. Mike was practically family. They'd been in and out of each other's houses so regularly as kids, their parents used to joke that they'd forget which one was theirs. "I guess," she said. "I'll go get you a few blankets—the couch folds out."

"That's okay," Mike said, slumping onto his side. "This is fine."

"I have to tell you," Jade said, smirking. "It's a good thing you didn't hook up with anyone tonight—because this is *not* attractive."

"Go away." Mike moaned, swatting at her blindly. His eyes were closed, and Jade guessed from the sound of his voice that he was already half asleep. She went to the linen closet in the hallway and grabbed a spare blanket, then came back and draped it over him. He mumbled something that sounded like,

"Thanks," rolled over, and was dead asleep in a matter of seconds.

"Some date," Jade muttered, laughing to herself. She turned off the lamp in the living room and went into the kitchen, where she wrote a quick note to her mom explaining that Mike was staying over. Then she taped the note to the hood above the stove and headed down the hall to her room.

What a night, she thought as she padded along the blue carpet. Here she was alone in an empty apartment with a guy, and he was sleeping on the couch. Okay, so it was Mike, who hardly qualified as a guy, but still. If her father could see her now, maybe he'd realize that Jade wasn't some immature kid that needed her mother home every minute of the day to make sure she was okay.

Then again, it didn't really matter what her father thought—he'd be back in Oregon soon, which was definitely for the best.

"So I'll call you tomorrow?" Ken asked, leaning down to kiss the top of Melissa's head. They were standing by her front door, and for some reason he felt anxious to say good-bye and get back home. It had been a long night.

Melissa nodded, not answering. She'd been pretty quiet all night—ever since the moment Maria had won the scholarship.

"Don't forget—you're going to have plenty of

other chances for a scholarship," he reminded her. "And they won't have all those crazy conditions either."

"I know," she said. She looked up at him, the corners of her mouth curving up slightly. "At least I know I got one vote," she said.

"Yeah," Ken said, smiling down at her. Then he pulled her close again so that his chin rested on her head.

"Besides, yours was the only one that mattered," Melissa added, her voice muffled by his sweater.

Ken sighed and held Melissa tight, rocking her back and forth. Slowly he flexed and loosened his jaw muscles, trying not to let his tension show. He knew he'd made the right decision by staying with Melissa, and tonight had only made him more certain. Sure, he'd been happy with Maria, but something inside him had always known that she'd be fine whether he was there beside her or not. But Melissa needed him, and he liked that.

And now that this whole scholarship thing was over, things could go back to normal between them.

Especially since the votes had been anonymous.

Ken Matthews

I have voted for Maria Slater because:

Maria deserves this award. It's that simple.

I mean, it seems obvious to me that all of the nominees are really smart and work really hard to get great grades. Plus they've all been involved in a ton of activities—things I didn't even know existed. But Maria's different. She doesn't do all that stuff just so she can add it to her college transcript. Sure, she wants to get into a good school and everything, but the difference is . . . Maria cares.

She cares about putting in her best effort, and she cares about doing the right thing. She cares about standing up for what she believes in, and she cares enough to do it even when it makes her unpopular. But most of all, Maria cares about making a difference in the world—making it a better place. And I guess that's why I think she deserves this scholarship. Because she will.

Jade sat up in bed on Saturday morning, rubbing her eyes. There had been voices yelling in her dream, and she was pretty sure one of them had been her father's, but the strange thing was that she could still hear it.

"*. . . leaving her alone at all hours of the night . . . strange boys sleeping over . . . you in and out of the hospital . . .*"

Suddenly it clicked in Jade's brain that the voices were real and that they were coming from the kitchen. She jumped out of bed and threw on her bathrobe, tying it as she ran down the hallway.

"What's going on—?" she started, but the sight of her father's furious face stopped her cold. "Dad—what are you doing here? I thought—"

"Go back to bed, Jade. This doesn't concern you," Mr. Wu said curtly. Jade's mother stepped out of the kitchen and stared wide-eyed at her daughter. She was still wearing the clothes she'd had on last night when she left for work, which meant she must have slept in them.

"But . . . w-what—," Jade stuttered, still unable to understand what was going on.

"Your father's flight was delayed," her mother explained. She paused, and Jade saw a flash of hurt in her mother's eyes.

Probably because she found out I lied to her, Jade thought, feeling sick.

"So he stopped by this morning for one last

good-bye," Ms. Wu continued, "and Mike answered the door."

Jade's eyes grew wide, and she clapped her hands to her mouth.

"They were . . ." Ms. Wu paused to narrow her eyes at Jade's father. "*Discussing* why Mike was here when I woke up, and I sent Mike home."

Jade flicked her gaze to her father, shaking her head. "It's not what you think. He wasn't feeling well and—"

"I've already heard the excuses, Jade," Mr. Wu said, "but as far as I'm concerned, there *is* no excuse for this. You need more supervision than you're receiving here."

"But Dad—Mike's like family," Jade protested. "You know that."

"I've seen and heard more than enough already," he replied.

Jade saw her mother flinch at his tone, and she practically lunged at her father. He had *no* right to accuse his ex-wife of not taking care of Jade when that was all she did.

"I will not have my teenage daughter living like this."

"John, she is not—"

"I told you," he interrupted, "I have heard enough." He straightened his shoulders, as if he were about to head into one of his important meetings. "She comes home to an empty apartment every day, invites boys to spend the night whenever she chooses, and you're so busy with work, you don't know the difference. Not to mention your health problems," he added.

Ms. Wu shot a confused glance at Jade, and Jade realized how this must seem to her mom—like Jade had confided all of these things to her father, complaining about her mom. He was using everything she'd said to try and *defend* her mom against Jade! She never should have told him anything about their lives. She never should have even let him in the door.

"I've been doing a lot of thinking since I've seen the way the two of you are living," Mr. Wu said.

Jade scowled. "You don't know what you're talking about," she snapped. She stepped closer to her mom, hoping she could somehow protect her against whatever her dad would say next.

"I think I do," Mr. Wu countered, shaking his head. "But the point is, things need to change. When we were first divorced," he said, turning to Jade's mother, "I was traveling quite frequently for my work, so it only made sense for you to get custody of Jade. Now, however, my trips are extremely rare, and I have a wife who is at home most of the time as well."

Ms. Wu's jaw hung open as her husband spoke, and Jade felt like the room was beginning to spin. This couldn't be real.

"Jade needs a stable home environment—not a

messy, small apartment with a mother who can't even take proper care of herself. Especially at a time like this, with Jade on the verge of college. She needs a responsible influence before it's too late."

Jade swallowed, moving even closer to her mother. She didn't want to believe what she was hearing. He could only be heading in one direction. *Don't say it,* she thought. *Don't say it.*

Mr. Wu glanced at Jade briefly, then fixed his gaze on her mother. "That's why I've decided to sue for custody of our daughter."

WILL SIMMONS

10:27 A.M.

When I get back to SVH, I'm going to show everyone that even on crutches, I'm a better quarterback than Ken Matthews. So much better that in a few weeks, everyone will stop calling him the "star quarterback" and start calling him "that guy who's standing in for Will Simmons." And when Melissa tries to trade up again, she'll be out of luck because I'm going to turn my back on her. Just like she did to me.

MELISSA FOX

10:29 A.M.

Ken's right. I'll have plenty of chances for scholarships. Who wants to go to a stupid East Coast school anyway? Only pretentious people like Maria. People who need to throw themselves into school because their social lives are nonexistent. Let her have her stupid college scholarship. I've got her boyfriend. And when she comes down from her little award-banquet high, she'll realize that I'm still way ahead.

JADE WU

10:49 A.M.

If my dad is actually serious about this, then he is in for the fight of his life.